"You goddamned officers ——
Detective Jay Austin bellowed. "You already
know that Colonel Lawrence is innocent, right?
How the hell do you figure that?"**

Colonel Alan Caldwell stopped at the curb. He reached in his jacket pocket for a cigar and started rolling it between his fingers to loosen the paper, all without taking his eyes off Austin. "In this country you're supposed to be innocent until proven guilty, boy," he said.

Nothing could have made Jay Austin madder. "Don't call me boy!" he yelled. "I'm no goddamned boy!"

Caldwell bit off a hunk of the cigar and reached for a match.

"Let's go talk to Lawrence," Austin said, biting back his temper.

Caldwell shook his head, puffing on the stogie to get it lit. "No way," he said. He squinted against the sun and pinned Austin with his steely eyes. Austin eyed him back, gritting his teeth, waiting him out.

"I'll get a warrant," Austin said finally.

"See how far you get trying to serve it on a federal military installation," Caldwell said. "Since you got here, you've been trying to piss on me. Like I'm some tree in a park. That's because you didn't think you needed me for anything. Well, suddenly it's a little different. . . ."

THE PRESIDIO

A NOVEL BY MIKE COGAN
BASED ON THE SCREENPLAY
WRITTEN BY LARRY FERGUSON

POCKET BOOKS

New York   London   Toronto   Sydney   Tokyo

Another *Original* publication of POCKET BOOKS

POCKET BOOKS, a division of Simon & Schuster Inc.
1230 Avenue of the Americas, New York, N.Y. 10020

ISBN: 0-671-66876-5

First Pocket Books printing June 1988

10 9 8 7 6 5 4 3 2 1

POCKET and colophon are trademarks of
Simon & Schuster Inc.

Printed in the U.S.A.

CHAPTER 1

PRESIDIO IS THE Spanish word for garrison, or fortified barracks. There's a good reason why the United States Sixth Army is headquartered in a fort with a Spanish name, and right in the most scenic part of the city of San Francisco, too.

In the spring of 1776, a couple of months before some rebellious British subjects back east signed their Declaration of Independence, Lt. Col. Juan Bautista de Anza, Lieutenant José Moraga, a friar, and a small party of soldiers came north from Monterey looking for sites for a fortress and a mission along the upper California coastline. The friar built his mission a mile or so away where the hills flatten out; it's still there, over on 16th and Dolores Streets, if you want to see it.

The brass found a site which had all the requirements of a good military fortification: proximity to one of the greatest natural harbors in the world, positioning up on the heights to make it defensible, plenty of trees for timber, plenty of pasture land for cattle, apparently endless fresh-water springs. That site is now the north central corner of the city of

San Francisco—1,698 acres of prime real estate overlooking the Pacific Ocean, the bay, and the narrow, fog-ridden strait called the Golden Gate.

One more historical note: along with the walls of the fort, one of the first buildings put up in the Presidio back in 1776 was the Officers' Club. It's still there, too—the oldest adobe building in San Francisco. Having survived Spanish, Mexican, and American soldiers for two hundred years, these old walls would tell you, if they could talk, that nothing ever changes.

Well, maybe some things. The MP who reported for duty in the wee hours of a dank, foggy night earlier this year was a woman. Her name was Patti Jean Lynch, and she was in her twenties, pretty in a farm-fed way, with "clean" written all over her. She maneuvered her little white Datsun into the parking lot behind the military police station and ran up the steps into the building. She had dark curly hair and the kind of healthy glow to her cheeks that your mother sent you outside to play for. Her face was pleasant and she was a no-nonsense kind of woman, on the level with anyone who leveled with her. The best kind of friend to have. She looked a lot younger than she was.

Patti Jean might have been heading for a dorm party in her clean greens and cozy, goose-down parka with the MP band on her arm, but the 9mm on her hip was serious. The heels of her regulation boots echoed loudly against the tile floor as she strode down the hallway, past posters showing military personnel in various uniforms, all at attention.

It was the late shift and the desks in the reception area were empty. Neat, no papers, all secured for

6

the night. Overhead fluorescents lit the place with a too-bright, phony daylight, invented by someone who had never taken a good look at the real thing. Patti Jean checked her wristwatch as she swung through the door into the dispatch room: five-thirty on the nose, plus five seconds. She looked up at the wall clock: five-thirty on the nose, plus five.

Patti Jean glanced briefly at the desk crew—the radioman and three MP's yakking it up about all the ladies they had made happy. Don't men ever talk about anything *interesting?* Patti Jean wondered idly.

"I ain't kidding, Colonel Grey's secretary can suck the chrome off a trailer hitch. Been hounding my ass for months—" That was Zeke, in his slow Mississippi drawl. Freckle-faced and tow-headed, he thought God had created him for the benefit of the female race. He shut off when he saw Patti Jean, ogling her with a down-home grin that was practically drooling. She ignored him as she came up to sign in.

The other MPs were Zeke's partner Al and a guy named Bud who never said much but had eyes that should have required a hunting license.

Pete, the Spec 4 dispatcher, sat in front of the radio with his earphones on, slurping coffee from a styrofoam cup. He was so skinny he always looked haggard, even skeletal, but the amount of chow he managed to stow away was legendary. It had even caused money to change hands when someone was dumb enough to bet he couldn't eat more than was humanly possible. Pete was talking to one of the cars, just giving them a "ten-four." He was a nice guy, but his eyes joined in the general review as Patti Jean passed by. What the hell, she knew it was part of the routine; it didn't bother her much any more. Once in a while she wondered what it might be like not to be hassled, though, just to get on with her job.

A warren of battery chargers was set on the wall under the clock, most of them plugged with hand-held radios getting their nightly boost. She picked one, tested it, got a satisfactory squawk. She signed it out.

"Joe called in sick," Pete told her. "I'm gonna put you on a desk tonight."

Patti Jean glanced over at him. "My ass, you are," she said.

Pete shook his head, then he smiled. "Okay, but stay on the radio," he said. "The fog's a real bitch."

"Name me an early morning when it wasn't," she told him. "I'll be okay."

"Right," Pete said, with a grin that was something like a salute.

Heavy boots sounded out in the hall, bouncing off the tiles. Four weary MP's came in to sign off duty. One of them tossed a handful of keys at Patti Jean. She caught them neatly.

"Spotted some activity earlier on the beach," he told her. "Out by Fort Mason." He stretched his neck in a left arc, then right, trying to smooth out the kinks.

"Like what?" Patti Jean asked.

"Oh, nothing, probably. Just a car cruising by, slowing up, goin' on. Nothing to stop anybody about. Only it's five o'clock in the morning. You know."

"Yeah. Anybody who's up at this hour must be nuts or up to no good. Or an MP," one of the guys doing backup duty said, sprawling out across two chairs.

"Or all three," his partner muttered. Nothing was worse than backup, just hanging around till someone else got in trouble and called for you.

"Okay," Patti Jean said. "Fort Mason. I'll check it out." She started for the door.

"Patti Jean?" It was Ole Mississippi. She turned around, waiting. "It gets cold out there, jest gimme a call," Zeke drawled.

She chose to treat him as if he were sane. "I've got a jacket," she said.

Zeke grinned wickedly. "Well, that's not the same as a man," he leered. Then he sneaked a look at his male audience, hoping for a laugh.

"Neither are you," Patti Jean told him. That got the laugh, and she had the satisfaction of seeing Zeke's boyish freckles disappearing under a deep red flush before she walked on out the door.

Without her partner, it was going to be a busy morning. She'd have to drive the patrol car, run the radio, and watch both sides of the road as well as the front and rear. And it was true that the fog was especially thick and high this morning; the temperature had dropped more than twenty degrees overnight. She slid behind the wheel, fired up the engine, and moved out of the parking lot onto Lincoln Boulevard. She picked up the car mike, reported in. "Unit One Foxtrot is ten-eight."

"Ten-four, One Foxtrot," Pete's voice came back cheerily.

She switched off, hung up the mike and turned the car west, toward the beach. Lincoln Boulevard is one of the arteries that meander across the wide Presidio grounds from east to west; for a while it takes a northerly jog and eventually joins up with Marine Drive, which is the nice wide scenic route to the ocean that the tourists take. Patti Jean loved this shift; at five-thirty in the morning, the wild expanses of countryside right in the heart of the city were silent and mysteriously shrouded in the salty-smelling fog that came up out of the Golden

Gate at night. The tall old trees were wrapped in blankets of soft white clouds. The frame houses along the drive slept peacefully; only the patrol car moved. All was still, and all was well. She thought briefly, as she always did, starting her rounds, of the generations of soldiers who had patrolled these very grounds while everyone else slept soundly under the fog blanket. It was good to feel a part of all those others—men, up till now—who watched so that others could sleep in peace.

Patti Jean was passing Fort Point, heading south along the rim high over the beach. Far out on the water, deep-throated fog horns could be heard baying to each other, sounding farther away than they were in the trick that fogs play. She heard the surf pounding against the rocky promontory a hundred feet below, crashing and roaring and receding only to crash and roar again, all the more wild and dramatic because it was invisible in the dense white swirls of fog. She slowed and drove by instinct down the winding road to the beach and the old fort.

As she neared the parking lot, Patti Jean heard angry voices grating on the peaceful stillness of the night. Car doors slammed, and then a car swung out of the lot and passed her. She got a fast glimpse of a huge and expensive American make, a Caddy or a Lincoln, and then it was gone into the fog.

"One Foxtrot to dispatch," she reported immediately. "Ten-eighty-six at Fort Point. Scared away a couple of lovebirds. Judging by the car, they could afford a nice hotel room."

Pete's voice came back: "Ten-four, Foxtrot."

"Think I'll have a look around," she said.

"Right. Stay on the hand-held, Patti Jean."

"Yes, daddy." Patti Jean grinned to herself. Pete was a good guy, and doing a good job. Watching out for the watchers. She picked up the hand-held radio, hauled open the door of the patrol car, and stepped out onto the clearing. With her other hand she grabbed the flashlight, flicked it around the area. Between the beach and the parking lot, wind-twisted trees leaned hard against the rocks. The surf was very near now, but still unseen, crashing down with a roar against the sands, eroding the earth beneath the time-weathered old building and the very ground where she stood. She shivered and hurried to the door of the building.

Her light picked up a broken padlock recently thrown onto the shifting sand. The old bunker loomed before her; her beam showed the door ajar. Two or three more steps brought her to the door; she kicked it open and shone her light inside. She punched the hand-held.

"One Foxtrot to Dispatch. Somebody tried to break in. Gonna need another padlock." Forcing herself to hang in there another minute or two, she flashed the light all around, into the corners, over the walls. Nothing she could pin down as having been messed with. "One Foxtrot," she said. "Securing here and returning to my vehicle."

She headed back to the cruiser and climbed inside. All was quiet again, and she circled up around past the Officers' Club. Something odd—there was a car parked in the rear parking lot. She peered through the fog but had to swing into the lot, park, and get out of her car to come up close enough to get a make. It was a giant '86 Lincoln, very likely the same car she had seen before. Both hands full of flashlight and hand-held radio, she approached cautiously. The car was empty. She checked the rear plate: UDW 137. It was quite a boat, sleek and new, although it could use a wash. It looked damn near big enough to serve as a troop carrier, although she was pretty sure that wasn't what it was doing on the base. But what, at this hour?

"One Foxtrot requesting a ten-twenty-eight, twenty-nine, on Uniform Delta Whiskey one-three-seven California plate," she called in.

After no more than two seconds' computer time, Pete was back to her. "One Foxtrot," he said, "your plate Uniform Delta Whiskey one-three-seven: no wants. 1984 Volkswagen van, registered to a Harold Owens, San Francisco."

Patti Jean's mouth dropped open. "Volkswagen?"

She studied the Lincoln. It had picked up a lot of mud on its wheels and underside. She peered more closely at the plate; it was splattered with globs of mud. She kicked at it with the toe of her boot, and the mud fell away: UDW 187. Parts of the eight had been obscured, so she'd read it like a three. She spoke low into the hand-held. "Ten-four," she said. "Checking further. I'll give you another call in a couple minutes."

She flashed her light around. The building was wrapped in thick white fog like a fine old woman settled down for the night in her woolly shawl. It seemed a pity to disturb her. But someone else had already trespassed here; the rear door was ajar.

Patti Jean reported, in a low voice that was almost a whisper: "One Foxtrot to Dispatch, 10-87. Checking an open door at Officers' Club."

Pete's voice took on a worrying note. "Ten-four," he responded, and then he warned her, "Stand by for Unit Two Bravo to back you up. Stay where you are, Patti Jean. Bud's leaving now."

Before she could acknowledge, there was a loud crash from inside the club. It reverberated against the silence of the fog-muffled morning; adrenalin immediately began pumping wildly through Patti Jean's slender body. She raced across the lot, hugged the wall near the door. She heard angry male voices inside. Her eyes fixed on the door. It had been jimmied. Shards of wood littered the ground. Patti Jean unholstered her gun. She slipped inside the building.

She was at the end of a narrow hallway. Her heart was doing a hundred and fifty. Down the hall there was a door, half open, leading into the kitchen. She stepped inside. Across the hall, another door led to what was probably a storeroom. Someone was shining a flashlight in there. She watched as it flicked under the doorsill, then retreated back inside the room. She figured two men, arguing in loud whispers. The flashlight crossed the doorway again. Patti Jean took a deep breath, then she charged across the hallway, kicked open the door, stood there, knees slightly bent, 9mm in both hands, firing position.

"Freeze!" she yelled.

The man with the flashlight beamed it toward her. And then something like a speeding freight train hit her full in the chest. Falling, she heard herself scream, but it got dimmer and faded away into silence before she hit the floor.

CHAPTER 2

Bud Meredith climbed into his patrol car and got it going all in one motion. Backup duty wasn't a whole hell of a lot of fun. Sometimes it meant just hanging out for eight hours, night after night, waiting for someone to need help, hoping they would and hoping they wouldn't. When they did, it was right away, pronto, this minute or sooner. He pushed hard on the accelerator and took Lincoln Boulevard in forty-five seconds flat, making the turn onto Sheridan on two wheels. Early rays of daylight were starting to cut through the fog, to lighten up the sky. The Officers' Club loomed up ahead of him, and he had his eye on it. Maybe that's why he didn't see the other car coming at top speed right for him, emerging from the fogbank like a screeching bat out of hell. Bud slammed his foot on the brake, but that wasn't going to do it. The Lincoln kept coming, king of the road, refusing to give, and this street wasn't going to be wide enough for both of them.

The patrol car swerved sharply to the right, crashing into a tree. Fishtailing, the Lincoln roared away. Bud rammed the gears into reverse, spun the

14

wheels. He wasn't going anywhere. Quickly, he reached for the radio mike. "Presidio. Unit One Boy," he yelled. "I have TC'd. I have TC'd. Suspect vehicle, '86 Lincoln southbound on Sheridan. Felony stop! Repeat—felony stop!"

Pete's voice betrayed excitement. "Ten-four, Unit One Boy. Will check you later."

Zeke and Al were about a mile away, cruising on a general lookout. Al was sipping at a steamy styro cup; Zeke was driving and chomping on a Butterfinger. When they heard Bud's call, Zeke turned the wheel for a "U," but before he could make it, the radar gun went bananas. Some insane bastard was coming down the hill behind them at ninety-four miles per hour. And there they were— crazed headlights cutting through the fog, cresting the hill and dropping down like all the "tilt" signs had just lit up. Tossing back the candy bar, Zeke spun the wheel around and slammed into gear.

"Some-bitch!" he muttered, deep-South indignant. The Lincoln roared past them at a speed the radar put at close to 100. Zeke stomped the gas and hit Bernard Avenue at full throttle. Wild-eyed, Al hung on, working the radio.

"We've got him!" he yelled into the mike. "He's heading for the Lombard Gate!"

Pete's steady voice came back strong. "One Boy, stay on the base. Zeke, you hear me? Do not pursue off base. SFPD is being notified, and they will respond."

"Shee-it," Zeke groaned, as he gave the gas pedal all he had. "We'll never catch him—less we head him off!"

As he said it, he did it, yanking the wheel in a sharp right turn. The patrol car jumped the curb, taking to the grass, scooping up mud and flowers and all that nice green stuff with it.

The avenue sweeps to the right just before it

leaves the Presidio. Giant fir trees and clumps of lush shrubbery border the wide meandering street. The grass has been lovingly tended by GI's for more than two hundred years. Of course it was a goner now, although Zeke did somehow manage to dodge all the trees and bushes that kept rising up before him. Clots of mud and topsoil flew in every direction as the cruiser made tracks through the manicured lawns. All was just beginning to be visible as the slow-breaking morning light cut through the deep night fog, with wispy white shreds still floating just above the uprooted earth.

It was close. Only a second too late. Zeke hit the pavement on Lombard, nearly scraping the paint off the Lincoln's back fender; he was that close. The patrol car fell into the wake as the huge machine punished its tires and howeled ahead. Lights flashing, brakes screeching, the MP's swung around and broadsided up against the Presidio wall just as the Lincoln thundered through the gate and out onto the city street.

Several blocks east, the night fog was still thick. A bit inland from the sea, the main part of the city remained fogbound longer than the Presidio's lofty heights, and there was about an inch of gauze still drifting around the street lights; everything looked black and white and shades of gray. A black and white cop car was parked behind a chopped Oldsmobile that had once been maroon. The two cops who were bringing down the dubious driver of that pile of junk were looking (and feeling) washed out at the tail end of this long night's shift. The driver leaning up against the cruiser had about as much zip as last week's mashed potatoes.

Officer Ralph Schmidt was checking out the kid's pockets. The usual collection of crud, plus a real interesting baggie about a third full of cocaine, tucked away in an inside vest pocket. Schmidt held it up with one hand, pinning the kid's eighteen-inch neck with the other.

"Well, now," he said. "What's this, Leroy? Your after-shave talc?"

"C'mon, pig," the pusher whined. "That shit ain't mine. I borrowed this vest."

The squawk box inside the black-and-white interrupted the chitchat. "Attention all units," said the crisp female voice. "Possible four-five-nine. Eighty-six Lincoln traveling east on Lombard. Presidio MPs request assistance."

"Let's hit it!" Dotson yelled. He was warming the passenger seat, monitoring the radio, and gesturing to Schmidt out the window. Schmidt rammed the baggie back into Leroy's vest pocket where he'd found it. He spun the kid like a top and cuffed him to the iron railing of a nearby fence.

"Catch you later, Leroy," he said over his shoulder as he raced to get into the car.

"Hey, that ain't legal, man!" Leroy hollered indignantly. Schmidt was going to give him the finger as he reached the street and turned to slide under the wheel, but he had to leap for his life as the giant Lincoln exploded out of nowhere, bearing down on him. Dragging open the door, Schmidt piled into the black-and-white and stood on the gas pedal. Rubber burned. Dotson hit the siren.

"Unit One Charlie Five, we are in pursuit of your Lincoln. East on Lombard at—" Dotson checked the radar gun "—sixty-eight miles per hour and climbing. Request code three pursuit," he yelled, eyeing his partner for agreement. Schmidt, already intent on chasing the son of a bitch, nodded without taking his eyes off the pavement as it flew past.

The corner of Laguna and Madison is one of

those freaky little San Francisco upgrades where the cable cars climb perpendicular to the earth, up, up, and away, much to the delight of the straphangers and the tourists. On the north side of that particular intersection, Laguna is flat. But immediately on the other side of Madison, the street turns straight up to head for the sky. The Lincoln cut through the fog clocking ninety. Sirens screaming, Schmidt and Dotson were just a block and a half behind.

Hurtling through the intersection, the Lincoln slammed into the bottom of the upgrade. The impact was awesome. Sparks billowed over the hood. Iron ripped into concrete with the force of the blow. Front hubcaps spewed in both directions, clattering and whirling like deadly gleaming Frisbees.

The Lincoln came down from its bounce, sailed through walls of fog, and landed about fifty feet up Laguna. The din of all that heavy metal crashing back down onto the cement made it seem likely the giant was mortally wounded, if not already dead. And if there was anybody inside that wasn't belted down, they were tossed salad now. Like Dotson, who hadn't had time to buckle up.

But before the cops got close enough to count the pieces, the mighty Lincoln started itself up again, and plowed ahead, trailing a piece of fender that sparked dangerously close to the gas tank. It kept on going, apparently unstoppable, a monster on wheels. Close behind, the black-and-white caromed into the intersection, about to hit the wall of upgrade at full throttle.

White-knuckling the wheel, Schmidt poured it on, faster and gaining. The speedometer needle circled eighty and kept on going. The car's frame was shimmying and shaking, vibrating with a rhythm all its own. Inside, Dotson was grabbing for the seat belt, but with all the swinging and swaying, he couldn't buckle himself in. And here came the wall that was Laguna Street, jutting up like a goddamned mirage in the mist, a bad dream he wasn't going to have time to wake up from.

"Oh, Jesus," he said, swearing and praying all in one, and then it hit. Without a belt, Dotson slammed hard up against the roof, cracking his head and neck with searing pain. Somehow, they were still moving, and fast. Schmidt turned the wheel sharply and, teetering for a long minute on the brink of turning over, the cruiser righted itself and roared up again. There were a few new clanks and clatters, and Dotson would be wearing a neck brace if they ever got out of this, but they were still in pursuit, and gaining.

The Lincoln wasn't looking nearly as spiffy as it had, but it was still moving at a fearful rate of speed. Hot on its trail, the black-and-white drifted into a wide parallel arc as they entered California Street. Both cars raced up the hill, in tandem now, engines roaring and chassis shaking. Dotson tried to get a look at the face of the driver, but his attention was abruptly diverted to a rear window, which had started to inch down. In the opening, the unmistakable cylops of a gun muzzle, pointing right between his eyes.

Dotson grabbed the radio, shouting into it to be heard against the decibels. "One Charlie Five," he identified himself. "Requesting Code three pursuit, damn it!"

Schmidt, maneuvering the wheel to dart and dodge the Lincoln, saw the gun and saw that it meant business. "Look out!" he yelled. But Dotson ducked too late. Death spit at him from the rear window of the Lincoln. His heavy body fell with the momentum of the bullet, thudding across Schmidt's lap, between his body and the steering wheel.

Schmidt frantically tried to push Dotson's dead weight back onto the passenger seat, but at ninety miles an hour, a 200-pound body on your lap can seriously impair your ability to cope. Out of control, the black-and-white became a deadly projectile. At the top of California street where it crests the hill, the two cars were neck and neck. But then the cruiser spun left, starting to corkscrew wildly down the hill. The Lincoln sped straight ahead, down Taylor and alongside the park, where the morning fog still hung in the brush. The park was deserted at this hour, and a very good thing, too. The cruiser blasted like a rocket missile gone crazy, spinning into the park, over the curb, rolling over and over, finally coming to a stop on its left side, cozied up against a newly painted bench.

For a moment, all was dead silent. Then a woman's voice: "One Charlie Five, come in." The voice gave way to static. Then: "Come in, One Charlie Five. Request status of your pursuit." Silence. A long silence. A wheel spun in the air. A thin tendril of ground fog nosed around the crushed logo of the SFPD on the side of the car. "Advise condition or cancel your pursuit," the voice ordered.

Her answer was an explosion that rattled windows for blocks. The black-and-white turned into a ball of flames; hell-hot fire seared the air. The sky turned black from the oily smoke, and the heat melted everything in its path.

The Lincoln never looked back.

CHAPTER 3

WHEN HIS BEEPER went off, it roused Jay Austin from a dreamless sleep.

"Hello!" he responded instinctively, sitting straight up. He was amazed to see that he was wearing one snakeskin boot. He was also wearing boxer shorts with Day-Glo red hearts splattered all over them. The unpleasant noise of the beeper was still grinding away at his brain, as insistent and unpleasant as a dentist's drill. "Oh, shit," he groaned. Even to himself, his voice sounded ragged, wrecked. His head hurt. He heaved himself slowly out of bed. Come to think of it, *most* of him hurt.

Jay Austin was not what you'd call good looking, exactly, but he was almost always sincere, and a little bit shaggy on top of it—a combination that seemed to interest women, even if only for the possibility of taming him. Not domesticating him; they never got that close. Just a brush and comb, and a jacket that matched his pants, and he might shape up into something you could take home and introduce to the folks. He had blue eyes and straight brown hair that always needed a trim. His features were irregular: a narrow nose that tilted up, ears on the big side but close to his head, firm upper lip and a full, passionate lower that gave him away. He was muscular and taut from regular workouts but some mornings, including this one, he could use a little help getting started.

Where the hell was the beeper? Who decided that beepers should have a vile, penetrating, headache-making, can't-wait-another-second yowling rasp? Why couldn't someone make those beepers a little nicer, a little gentler, a little less painful to the hung-over ear . . . and where *was* the fucker, anyway?

Jay looked around the room with the one baby blue eye he had managed to get open. There was the other snakeskin boot, right in the middle of the floor. And his jeans nearby. He looked around the room. Something suspicious in the basketball hoop? Could he make it clear across the room to check it out? He moved his legs slowly over the side of the bed. He grabbed his aching head. He tried standing up.

He made it to the hoop, reached up painfully and felt around inside it. Yes. Good reflex thinking, Austin, even when the conscious mind is blotto. The silence was blessed. There was something caught in the mesh basket up there besides the beeper. He pulled it out and examined his catch. One beeper, one brassiere. Austin smiled— memory coming back?—and tossed the bra back into the hoop with an overhand tip. Gently, he maneuvered his wracked body back to bed, not to lie down—which he was more than willing to do—but to perch on the edge and call in. He picked up the phone and dialed.

"This is Austin," he said, a little hoarsely. "Whaddaya want?"

"Chief wants to talk to you, Jay. Hang on."

"Austin? Didn't you used to be Army? Stationed out at the Presidio, right?"

The chief had a voice that sounded mad even when he wasn't, so how could you ever know? Austin checked his watch. He dragged open the drawer of the bedside table and let his eyes check his Browning while he talked. "Yeah. I was stationed out there, why?"

"We need somebody who knows the area, knows the drill out there, to work with a Lieutenant Colonel Caldwell—"

"Oh, wait a minute, Chief, have you ever got the wrong—"

"You *were* stationed out there, no more'n a year or so ago, right?" the Chief barked.

"Well, yes, but—"

"No 'buts,' Austin, except for your butt which you will haul out there as fast as you can."

"Okay, okay. You're the boss."

"Report to this Lieutenant Colonel Caldwell; you'll find him at the Officers' Club, which is the scene of the crime. Get there in the next half hour or less. How long will it take you?"

"I'll be as quick as I can."

"What do you mean as quick as you can? What the hell is that supposed to mean?" the chief roared.

"Because I just woke up, and I'm not exactly sure where I am, asshole." He slammed down the receiver—that was a mistake; the noise was deafening. He got to his feet again, looked around the room. Okay. Find the john, throw cold water on it, he'd make it. He headed, surely but unsteadily, for a door that opened off the bedroom.

He was almost blinded by the glare—gleaming white tiles, flourescent lights, white tub and shower curtain. He looked in the mirror—mistake. He

23

shut his eyes, reached behind the shower curtain, and turned on the water full blast.

A woman screamed.

Austin's eyes flew open and he ripped back the shower curtain. Sitting in the bathtub under the full streaming water was a terrific-looking blond lady. The only thing she was wearing was his shoulder holster around her neck.

"Who the hell are you?" he blurted out, although it was probably not the most polite thing he could have said under the circumstances.

"Turn it off!" she yelped. Her lush hair was soaked, clinging very prettily to her head and neck and shoulders. Everything about her seemed to be very well put together indeed.

Austin turned off the water. That helped him get a better look. The lady was gorgeous. A pair of wide blue eyes, everything else in pairs also looking mighty good. A million perfect white teeth—she was laughing now.

"Uh—sorry I interrupted your bath," he stammered.

"It's okay, I was just surprised," she laughed.

"You're wearing my holster," he pointed out inanely.

"I was cold and you put this on my neck. You said it was where you kept your heater," she prodded, but his mind stayed blank on that particular episode.

"I did?"

"You did." She laughed again. "Then I showed you where I kept my heater," she said.

Austin frowned. He hated blank spaces in his life. "Where am I?" he asked her.

She stopped laughing. In fact, she looked alarmed. "Isn't this *your* place?" she asked. "You swore this was your place!"

Austin rubbed his temples. He wished she would get out of the tub and let him take his shower. "Well, then, I guess it must be my place," he said.

She laughed again, then stood up and reached for a towel. For a mad moment, as she bent over, drying herself, Austin considered rerunning what must have happened last night, only this time he'd have his head together and he'd remember it, too—but duty called. He settled for an appreciative glance or two, then he pulled the plug and let the water run out of the tub, turned on the shower to cold and forced himself to step inside. The blond lady was dried and dressed and thoughtfully gone when he came out. His holster was lying on the rug, but it was pretty damp. He stuck the Browning in an inside pocket and hoped nobody would ask how come. He didn't take time for a shave.

Jay Austin was behind the wheel of his Dodge and into the morning rush-hour traffic within twenty minutes of the beeper call. He knew he was pushing his life a bit too speedily these days, only getting away with it because he was still in his twenties. One of these years he'd definitely have to slow down, maybe even settle down. Fat chance! He liked his life. Just the way it was, mystery blondes in the bathtub and all. And his head was clear now; he felt fine and feisty. He listened to some police calls on the radio as he turned toward the Presidio.

He nosed the Dodge through the gate with mixed feelings. He wouldn't want anybody to know it, but his heart still beat faster when he checked out the symbols carved into the stone columns on either side of the gate: Infantry . . . Artillery . . . Cavalry . . . and the Great Seal of the United States of America. He took the slow curve and his eyes caught something that looked out of place: someone had recently torn up a deep swath through the lawn here, between the towering fir trees. Slowing down to take a look, Austin figured no more than a couple of hours since the dew-spangled grass had gone belly-up. Either some GI was going to catch thirty days for driving drunk and destroying government property, or this had something to do with why he was here.

He turned off at the Officers' Club and parked in the lot. It was busy this morning: MP cars with their radios blaring and red lights spinning—he counted three. MP's standing around, warming themselves in the sun after a cold night, looking glum and angry. He spotted a face he knew and walked over to him.

"Hey, Zeke," Austin said. He noted the Spec 4 was trying to light a cigarette with hands that shook bad. And the guy's face looked like a plate of lima beans—green and wrinkled. "How's it hanging?" Austin asked quietly.

Zeke looked at him in surprise, doing a double take. "Austin?" He seemed to be in some kind of shock, Austin thought, as he nodded. "What the hell are you doing here?" Zeke asked him.

Austin showed him the badge that said he was an inspector with the San Francisco Police Department.

"No shit?" Zeke said. He was definitely slow on the uptake today, even for himself.

"No shit," Austin told him. "So what's the story?" he asked. "Some officer shoot himself in the foot?"

"You don't know? They didn't tell you?" Austin shook his head, no. Zeke was having trouble figuring it all out. "You mean they sent you over here and you don't even know why yet?"

"Something like that," Austin said. "So what happened, Zeke?"

"Oh, God," Zeke sighed. He looked at Austin as if sizing up whether he could take it and then delivered the knockout. "It's Patti Jean," he said.

Austin's grin froze on his face. They stood there for a minute, face to face, one feeling worse than the other.

"I'm sorry, Jay," Zeke said finally. "She never had a chance." He shuffled his feet. "If there's anything—"

"The old man inside?" Austin interrupted coldly. He felt like stone, cold, dead stone. Patti Jean . . .

Zeke nodded and made way for Austin to walk past him and on into the back door of the club.

There was a blizzard of activity inside the narrow little hall. A swarm of CID guys in suits. Forensic experts were dusting everything for prints. Grimfaced, Austin shouldered his way through to the open door of a storeroom where another clot of military and federal drones were buzzing around.

A coroner's aide was snapping pictures of what used to be Patti Jean, sprawled on the floor on her back. Austin looked, and was sorry he had. He ground his teeth, trying not to let out a goddamned sob. She had been a good partner, a good friend.

A civilian, a rumpled man in his thirties, clutching a clipboard in the crook of his arm, was sweating profusely and talking to a wideshouldered colonel with a full board of ribbons on his chest, topped by combat Infantry Badge and Airborne Insignia. Austin wanted to look anywhere but at Patti Jean—even if it meant getting closer to the Provost. He moved in close enough to catch the conversation. Lt. Col. Caldwell seemed to be staring down at the dirt in one of two oversized potted palms. It had been freshly watered. Automatically, Austin's eye checked out the other tree. That was odd; it appeared bone dry. He tuned into the conversation.

"It's a kentia palm, sir," the civilian was saying, in an anxious tone. "It's very—"

Caldwell cut him off. "I don't care what it's called, Mueller. When did you water it?" he barked.

Caldwell was a real pain in the ass. Austin couldn't stand the sound of his voice; it was worse than the goddamned beeper. The colonel had a slight accent, an upward English or Irish tilt to his voice, sounded like he was better than anybody, that kind of accent. Even when you knew somebody couldn't help it, that he had been born with it, you wanted to punch him in the nose when he talked that way, especially if he was bucking for an eagle on his shoulder and shoved it at you every chance he got. Caldwell kept himself in terrific shape. He had probably once been handsome, maybe still was, to some people. His sandy hair was sparser by a few years, in fact he was egglike on top, and the rest had gone mostly gray. But his eyes always seemed to be looking right through you, thinking their own private thoughts. His mustache was full and a lot browner than his hair, trimmed to military precision. Caldwell was one hell of a career man—the kind who could frighten the enemy with a sneer and save on bullets.

But this was a SFPD matter, and Austin was in charge. It was about time he let old Caldwell know it. He stepped up to the two men and, turning his back to Caldwell, asked the guy in the slacks and polyester jacket, "Who are you?"

"John Mueller, sir," the civilian answered nervously. "I manage the NCO Club."

"You checked the inventory, Mueller?" Austin asked as he nodded at the clipboard. He wasn't the least bit sure what the hell was going on here, but he was letting everybody know he was firmly in charge. The colonel was gratifyingly quiet all of a sudden.

"Yes, sir, I checked everything," Mueller was saying. "But there's nothing of any value in here to steal. Just supplies, that's all."

"Bullshit," Austin said. "Somebody wanted something." He nodded over in the direction of Patti Jean's body. "There's a girl lying over there shot full of goddamn holes!" he said with more passion than he intended.

"Yessir," Mueller said, almost visibly cowering.

"Don't call me 'sir,' Mueller!" Austin barked. "People that you call 'sir' got crap for brains!" He turned to Caldwell and looked straight into the old man's face. Damn, he had forgotten about Caldwell's smirk, that permanent disfigurement of the mouth that made you feel like you were in the wrong army. Always long on the bravado, Austin sneered, "Ain't that right—*sir?*"

Caldwell stuck a gnawed old cigar under his mustache and chomped on it instead of saying what was obviously on his mind. Mueller's eyebrows crawled around on his fleshy face. He looked from one to the other—the young buck challenging the one with all the antlers and apparently getting him to back down. Working for the Army was a bitch; there were always all kinds of things going on that a normal person couldn't figure.

"So, did you find anything missing, Mueller?" Austin asked again.

"No, sir. I mean, no, I didn't. The rear door's been jimmied."

Austin nodded. "Yeah, I noticed that." With a movement of his hand, he dismissed Mueller for now. When the manager had left the room, Austin glanced back at Patti Jean. "I want the asshole who did this," he said quietly. "I want him real bad." He looked Caldwell in the eye again, man to man.

"You do," Caldwell finally said with some sarcasm.

Austin studied his former commander as if seeing him for the very first time. "I got some news for you," he said. "What we have here is a multijurisdictional investigation, requiring the cooperation of the Army *and* the San Francisco Police."

Caldwell continued to look down on him from on high. He wasn't that much taller than Austin, but he carried himself as if he were, and got away with it.

"I'm the police part," Austin went on. "As far as the Army goes, CID handles felonies, don't they?" He moved closer to Caldwell. "If I'm not mistaken, you're just a provost marshal. Aren't you . . . *sir?*"

Caldwell stood like stone. "Are you done?" he clipped off with his trace of superior accent.

"Maybe," Austin conceded belligerently.

Caldwell took a deep breath, as if bored or world-weary. He wound up and let go: "Now listen, boy. I was prepared to cut you a little slack, because of Patti Jean. So I let you do your Dirty Harry imitation for a few minutes. Your time is up, so listen real good to what I'm going to tell you. This is my command here. You watch your mouth when you're here . . . or I just might cut your balls off and serve them for breakfast." He paused, letting it sink in. "Do you understand me?" he finished.

Austin nodded. "Oh, yeah," he said.

Caldwell turned on his heel and left the little storeroom. Austin moved over to the wall and examined the potted palms. His first impression had been correct: one was dry as a desert; the other dark and moist, freshly watered. He pried some of the damp soil loose. Holding it between his fingers, he sniffed at it. Nothing special, nothing but wet dirt.

He went out into the hall, stepping carefully around the group still examining Patti Jean's body. He spotted the manager and called out to him. "Hey, Mueller. Did you water one of those plants?"

Mueller frowned and shook his head. The CIDs and homicide squads from both the Army and the city were milling around together now, and the place was getting crowded. Austin got out of there and headed back to headquarters, where he could start trying to put the pieces together. Next time he faced Caldwell there had to be more than sarcasm between them. If it had been anyone besides Patti Jean, he would figure a way to be relieved of this one, but he was mad and sad and ready to do whatever was needed to find out who did this to her. Even cooperate with King Caldwell, the Royal Pain in the Arse.

Austin calmed down by the time he reached his own headquarters building. It was clean and new and, well—*civilian*. He hit the elevator button for the sixth floor and stepped out feeling hopeful. Some of the breaks had to go his way. Law of averages, if not law of smarts.

As soon as his captain had filled him in on the horrors of the morning, Austin headed for Ballistics.

He strolled through the outer offices, saying hello to all the desk jockeys, and pulled up at the lab receptionist's desk.

"Hi, Jay," the pretty young woman there greeted him. "Hulse is waiting for you."

"Great, thanks," Austin said as he swung past her and through the door to Hulse's office.

"Who do you know who's Russian?" Hulse asked the minute he saw Austin. Theo Hulse was a huge man, broad and almost round. He had a graying mustache that twined around like Mark Twain's. He dressed spiffily and fancied himself a detective. What he really was was the best ballistics man in the west.

"Russian?" Austin echoed. "Uh, let's see . . . Lenin. Marx. Stalin. Gorbachev?"

"Close but no cigar. Who do you know in San Francisco now who's Russian?"

"Hey, Hulse, if this is a joke, save it for a minute. Did you get any results on the bullets that killed Patti Jean?"

"Aw, shit, Jay, I'm sorry. She used to be your partner, when you were out there, didn't she? Hell, I didn't mean to kid you. I'm really sorry."

"Yeah, so . . . you got any answers?"

Hulse's natural enthusiasm and bubble buoyed him up again; he was not a man who could stay glum for long, probably a good thing in his occupation. "That's what I was referring to," he said. "The gun was a Tokarev. Thirty-three. Russian. Got any ideas who it might belong to?"

Austin's eyes widened. "Tokarev . . . that shouldn't be too hard to trace. Maybe I'm getting a spot of luck today after all."

"Good. I'm glad. If I can be of any help, you know, cheering you up? Finding the slob that did it. She must have been a real nice girl," Hulse said.

"Yeah. How about the other bullet—the one they dug out of Dotson's skull?"

"Jeez, poor old Dotson, wasn't that a crime! Yeah, how about that—the same gun."

"The same gun?"

"Right. The same Tokarev 33 got both your old partner and one of ours. Shit."

"Thanks, Hulse. Thanks very much."

"Any time. Say, who the fuck would have a Russian gun? You got any ideas?"

"Maybe." Austin told him. "Maybe it was a war souvenir."

"Good thinking," Hulse told him, admiringly. "No kidding. You're a good inspector, Inspector."

"Thanks. You're not so bad yourself."

"Get 'em, Jay. They killed your partner, and they killed two of ours."

Austin nodded. "We'll get 'em."

He was in such a rush to get back to the Presidio that he considered turning on his siren, but he was supposed to be unmarked and how long could an ordinary blue Dodge stay ordinary if it went around town blasting all the time. He controlled his anxiety as best he could, but all the same the tires squealed when he pulled up in front of the firing range.

Things were not anywhere near as friendly there. He had to deal with a certain Sgt. Garfield who proved to be a real wooden Indian. Nothing. Not without a direct order from—guess who? This was going to be a bitch; he'd have to work through Caldwell and with Caldwell every step of the way. And that didn't leave him much of anywhere.

CHAPTER 4

He cruised his sky blue Dodge down Long Avenue, the tree-lined street that housed the ghosts of Sherman, MacArthur, and Pershing—plus a few Mexican and Spanish generals—and now some live officers and their families, too. On his left, looking down a grassy slope, he saw the Parade grounds, then the old adobe Officers' Club, and the Army Museum. On his right, he checked the nameplates as he passed slowly by the white frame houses, most with pleasant porches and some with kids' swings and tricycles out on the lawn. Finally he saw the tag he was looking for: LT. COL. A. CALDWELL. He pulled to the curb and climbed the steps.

The young woman who opened the door in response to his knock had the warmest grin he'd ever fallen into by surprise. A couple of centuries crawled by while Austin checked out her tumble of natural blond hair and the definite welcome in her greenish eyes. They were bright hazel green, he figured. A very rare and beautiful color for eyes. Something like hot pulsars were working in his chest; all he could do was wonder how this ravishing creature had happened to land on earth. And what a lucky break that he was there, too . . . even though he didn't seem to be able to speak just now.

When she spoke, her voice was all money and marmalade. "Say something." And she smiled at him again.

"What?" was all he could croak out.

She was still smiling. "That's a start," she said.

Austin gulped and wondered how come he had gone backward in time and become a teenage jerk. Again. "I'm Inspector Jay Austin. San Francisco Police Department. Who are you?" There, who said he couldn't speak? Just the facts, just stick to the facts. I love you, ma'am. I've never seen anything so pretty as you in my whole life.

"You didn't do that right," she said. She was still smiling and it would melt an igloo.

"I didn't?" he shot back. Brilliant.

"No. You're supposed to show me your ID." She was mocking him, but that was all right, as long as she just kept standing there and let him look at her.

Austin pulled himself together, finally. "Close the door," he said.

"What?"

He waited, and she shrugged and shut the door. Austin whipped his wallet out of his pocket with one hand, knocking with the other. She opened it, trying not to smile now. Instead of his face, she saw his wallet open to the badge and ID. He lowered it. "Hi! I'm Inspector Jay Austin—San Francisco Police Department."

"Much better," she approved.

"I'm looking for Colonel Caldwell."

"This is where he lives. He works someplace else."

Austin grinned. "I kind of figured that."

A bunch of whooping GI's rode by in a utility

truck, rumbling and hooting like Mardi Gras in New Orleans. Austin didn't even hear them.

"You want to wait on the porch, Inspector Jay Austin?" the beautiful young woman teased.

"Maybe I'd better come in," he said.

He followed her inside, hoping without much real hope that Beauty would turn out not to be related to the Beast. She didn't look like him, that was for damn sure.

The interior of the old frame house was regulation but homey, as far as Austin noticed. His concentration was preempted by the extraordinary body leading him in. The rest of her was as perfect as her face. He followed her hips into the foyer. He was totally under the spell of this lady's looks, so his police training switched onto automatic: some part of his brain registered a living room opening off to the left and a dining room on the right, and opposite the door about twelve feet across the foyer there was a staircase going up to the second floor.

She started to lead him into the living room but evidentally thought better of it. She stopped and turned back to him. "Coffee's hot," she said. "Want some?"

He just stared at her.

"Donna Caldwell," she said. "I'm the daughter."

Austin nodded. "Absolutely," he answered inanely.

At least he made her laugh. She turned into the dining room and he followed her around the long oval table, past cheerful rose-and-brown wallpaper and a row of English hunting lithographs, into the bright white kitchen. He noted that she looked great against any background, warm or cold. There was a cozy little table for two in front of the kitchen window, looking out over the golf course and its impeccably landscaped fairways, greens, and traps.

He hoped they were going to sit there, where the sunlight would shine on her and they'd be close enough to touch each other, just in case either of them should want to.

Donna went to the stove, poured two mugs of coffee from an old-fashioned pot. Over her shoulder, she asked, "Are you here about the MP who was killed last night?"

"Yeah." He stood watching her.

"Our phone's been ringing off the hook this morning." She handed him a steaming mug and led him to the little table. The sun lit up her hair just as he had known it would. It looked like the effect all the old masters had been after when they tried to give their women a special glow. He shook himself mentally and concentrated on what she was saying. He liked the way her mouth moved. "The Presidio is a small post," she said. "Never any excitement. So when this happened, everybody had to talk it over with everybody else. My father hasn't talked to me about it, though. I can't tell you anything, if that's what you want."

"No. That's okay. That's fine. I mean, I have to see him. I've already seen him, but I have to see him again. Anyway, I know what you mean about how small the place is," Austin said. "I used to be an MP here, a few years back. As a matter of fact, I was in your father's command. But I don't remember anybody mentioning that he had a daughter." He leaned forward, frankly admiring her.

Unrattled by his ogling, Donna took a sip of coffee. "I was away at school," she said. "I only came back last month."

A compatible silence came over them and it was nice, sitting there in her kitchen, watching the sun caress her hair and her skin, sipping good coffee and wondering if he could really handle this situation. He knew how badly he wanted her; but what was he getting himself in for?

"Why did you leave the Army?" Donna asked.

He shrugged. "I had my reasons."

She peered at him over the rim of her cup. "Was my father one of them?"

He took a long sip of coffee instead of answering her. It was good coffee, better than the instant shit he had gotten used to. He put the cup down and looked at her again. Her looks hit him again, wham in the pit of his stomach.

"Hey," he said, in spite of himself, "you're pretty."

"Oh." Donna got up and went over to the stove, brought the pot back to refill both cups. He waited; it was her move. She took the pot back and put it on the slow burner. When she came back and sat down again she had an innocent look on her face that should have told him she was up to something, not that he knew her that well yet. She just asked, out of the blue, "Is it hard?"

He managed not to choke on his coffee. "Is what hard?" he countered.

"Being a cop," she said, looking him straight in the big blues.

"Oh." Here goes. "Well, I can't remember it ever being as hard as it is right now," he told her solemnly.

She laughed. It was a wonderful sound, spontaneous and free and completely seductive. She was a no-bullshit lady; he couldn't believe his luck.

"Inspector Austin," she said, still laughing, "are you flirting with me?"

"I thought it was the other way around," he retorted. Then he got serious, because all of a sudden he was afraid he might not stay this lucky.

"Listen," he said, "your father's going to tell you all kinds of things about me."

"What kind of things?"

He reached across the little table and touched one of her fingers with one of his. "Not the good kind," he said.

She didn't move away. "Are they true?" she asked him.

"Find out for yourself," he challenged her. "Have dinner with me tonight."

She grinned. "You don't waste much time."

His voice took on an urgent note. "How do I get hold of you without going through your father?" he asked.

She let him know he was really speeding. "Maybe I should have made decaf," she said.

He loved her—she was great, she was lovely and funny and quick and in a minute she'd be wanting him as much as he wanted her, he could feel it, he knew she would, he hoped with all his heart she would. "Look," he told her urgently, "your old man is going to come home any minute. He's going to stroll in here and find us talking. He's an intelligent guy, he'll notice right off the electricity between us."

"Electricity?"

Austin nodded. "Right. How attracted you are to me. That'll have him climbing the walls in no time. Later, when he gets you alone, he'll tell you what a jerk I am and order you to stay away from me."

Donna withdrew her fingers from his, picked up her coffee mug, holding it lightly with both hands. "My father doesn't order me to do anything. We have an agreement," she told him.

"He'll break it," Austin said. He knew damned well he was right. What luck, her being Caldwell's daughter. He couldn't figure out whether he had a chance or not. If he could still read vibes, she wanted him nearly as badly as he wanted her, but Daddy-o was something else.

"No, he won't. We made our agreement when I was seven years old. And he hasn't broken it yet," Donna told him.

Austin smiled. "You were never seven years old." She smiled. How did teeth ever get that perfect? He was encouraged. "Are you free tonight?" he asked again.

"I don't believe this," she said.

"Believe it." He dug in his pocket for his wallet and a ballpoint. "Here—here's my business card. Call me this afternoon and we'll arrange a time. I'll write my home address and number on it, too. Just in case." He scribbled on the back of the little white card. He knew what she was thinking, or hoped he did: that here was a sort of good-looking fellow, well, in a rugged sort of way. And he hoped she was thinking that his being brash and even a little pushy was very exciting—well, maybe a little exciting, interesting, anyway, enough to take it a bit further. A lot further. He handed her the card.

They were looking silently into each other's eyes when the colonel walked in. He headed straight for Donna with a big smile, but he stopped in his tracks and so did the smile when he spotted who was sitting at the table with her. He seemed very tall when you were sitting down. He was still a hell of a handsome guy despite the bald pate, Austin conceded, and probably still sexy to some ladies. But what he gave out mostly was military bearing, unbendable spine, taut jaw held high, mustache in perfect trim. There was something about him, some lingering touch of whatever he was that stank of the days when class meant something, when there was an empire to rule over with a stick and a tough-guy attitude. In a way, Caldwell's looks and know-it-all eyes revealed that he must have had some high old times in his day; but on the other hand, to Austin right this minute the guy looked like he'd never cracked a real smile in his life. It wasn't pretty to be stared down this way when you were sitting in the guy's own kitchen with his own luscious daughter. Austin felt like he'd been caught with his pants down; for once he couldn't think of anything to say. Then Donna got up from her chair, taking her coffee mug and (hallelulah) Austin's card.

"Hi, Dad. Remember Jay Austin?" she said by way of introduction.

Caldwell nodded curtly. There are lots of ways of not smiling; his was unique. When Lt. Col. Caldwell was not smiling, the whole world was supposed to tremble in its boots. He was not smiling now. "I remember," he snapped.

Donna headed for the door. "He remembers you, too," she said. Then she was gone.

Caldwell's lack of a smile turned into a polished-brass frown. "What are you doing in my house?" he demanded. His lips were tight and his voice just barely this side of menacing.

Austin tried to remember. Now that she was out of the room, it was possible to concentrate again. Oh, yes. "I got the ballistics report on the weapon used on the patrolman who was shot in the pursuit this morning. Matches the slugs in Patti Jean."

"So?"

He was right, it wasn't exactly news that the same jokers in the '86 Lincoln had something to do with Patti Jean's death and poor Dotson's, too. But there *was* something Caldwell didn't know. "They all came from a Tokarev 33," Austin told him.

"Russian," Caldwell noted. He moved to the stove, poured himself a cup of coffee. Austin was fidgeting and suddenly felt silly sitting at that dainty little table all by himself. He stood up, set his empty cup down on a counter.

The colonel turned from the stove, stood ramrod-straight and stared Austin down. He wasn't belligerent so much as he was calm, intelligent, and—goddamn it—superior. "What do you want?" he asked Austin finally.

"I could use your help, and I thought it was best if we didn't go through channels," Austin told him straight out. "My instincts tell me the Tokarev belongs to someone on the base."

"Your instincts suck," Caldwell snorted. "It could belong to anybody. The base is open to the public. Anybody can drive in here and you know that. We're on the Forty-nine Mile Scenic Drive. Anybody could bring a gun in here. A Russian gun might even belong to a Russian. They have a consulate in San Francisco, you know."

Austin nodded. "Or it might belong to somebody who served in 'Nam and picked it up as a war trophy," he said calmly. He felt better talking business, knowing where he stood and what was on the colonel's mind.

They both knew that was more likely. Odds are high that there are more vets with illegal souvenirs hidden in a dresser drawer under their socks and shorts than there are gun-toting Russians in this country. It just figures. The spit-and-polish provost marshal and the civvy inspector stared each other down. Neither wavered this time; Jay Austin was back in control. He'd only lost it for a minute. What was a—a—an *officer*—doing with such a terrific daughter, anyhow? It was enough to throw anybody off the track. But he was back on it now, and eyeballing the colonel as coolly as you please. A standoff.

Out on the sun-splattered golf course, some guy all dressed up in tartan plaid pants was teeing up.

Caldwell's voice was clipped and chilly. "I'm only going to ask you one more time. What do you want?"

"I talked to a Sergeant Garfield in the arms room this morning," Austin told him. "When I asked him if he knew of anybody on the base who had a Tokarev, he said he might." Austin spoke carefully, knowing he was going to antagonize the old bastard. It was the last thing Austin wanted to do now, but he had to have the colonel's cooperation. In a couple of ways, come to think of it, but duty before passion. "When I tried to get more information, the sergeant got amnesia and threw a bunch of red tape in my face," he said.

Caldwell took it in. "And you want me to help you with Garfield?"

Austin nodded. But he knew it wasn't going to be this easy.

"A couple of hours ago," Caldwell said with ice in his voice, "you only wanted to deal with CID. I was just a provost marshal." He stood there and waited for Austin to squirm. If he'd known anything about Jay Austin, he wouldn't have waited.

"Tell you what," Austin said. He turned to go. "Forget it."

"Wait."

He turned back. Caldwell studied him for a long minute. They stood there with about three feet of yellow linoleum between them and then the colonel made up his mind. "Let's go," he said. He set his coffee mug in the sink, grabbed his cap and headed for the door, letting Austin bring up the slack behind him.

No sign of Donna as they crossed through the foyer and out the door. The huge old elms on the lawn cut the bright sun and the air had turned warm. Without breaking step, Caldwell hauled himself into the passenger seat of Austin's Dodge. Austin went around, slid behind the wheel and revved up, heading back to the pistol range. They didn't waste any more words on each other.

CHAPTER 5

ENCLOSED IN AN eight-foot high cyclone fence, the range sat high on a hill overlooking the parade grounds. Austin pulled up at the parking lot. Caldwell got out and strode ahead into the square windowless brick armory building. The anteroom had military posters all along the walls and hard benches to sit on if you had to wait. A Dutch door with the top half open and the bottom half shut led to an office with a couple of desks and a rear wall lined with racks and racks of weapons, all types. Iron rings were bolted to the floor in several places, as well as the wall, and huge padlocks secured the gun racks. Over the Dutch door, a couple of names were stenciled on regulation signs. Sgt. P. Garfield, SP4 was one of the names; the creature himself sat at the first desk with his hair slicked back and his lips moving, reading a comic book.

When Caldwell approached the Dutch door, the sergeant looked up and immediately slammed the magazine shut, leaping to attention. "Afternoon, sir," he snapped.

Caldwell jerked a thumb in the general direction of the civilian coming up behind him. "This is Inspector Austin, San Francisco Police," he said.

Garfield eyed Austin suspiciously.

"We've met," Austin said.

The sergeant glanced at his boss. Caldwell stood impassive, his chin high and his expression one of boredom, waiting for the noncom to figure it out. Garfield flicked his pig-eyes back to Austin. Not that he was going to give over, just like that. Maybe the colonel was playing some kind of game, testing him. He didn't like civilians coming in here asking questions and telling the Army what to do. "Yeah?"

"You got a Tokarev stored here?" Austin asked him. "I asked you that before, remember?" he prompted.

The sergeant looked over at the colonel again. This time Caldwell nodded curtly, just once, eyes forward, straight-line mouth under the shade of his mustache not giving away a damn thing. The nod meant it was okay for Garfield to talk, so he did.

"Nope."

Austin shifted his weight from one foot to the other, bored and irritated at this familiar buck-passing routine. "When I talked to you before, you said you might have some information for me," he reminded Garfield.

The sergeant scratched his ear with a pencil. "That's right," he allowed, "but you didn't ask me for any information just now. You asked me if the weapon was stored here."

Austin gritted his teeth. "Oh, this is fun. Yeah, I'm having fun!" he snarled. The sergeant blinked, innocent. And stupid. Covering his ass. "All right," Austin said, pulling out some patience from his very low reserve. He spoke as one might to a small backward child, "What information do you have about a Tokarev 33, Sergeant Garfield?"

Again the sergeant looked at Caldwell. The colonel, unsmiling, patient, gave a nod. It was like a ventriloquist act; Austin had been long enough out of the Army to forget what it was like dealing with noncom-poops. His teeth were going to be ground down to stubs by the time Garfield let it out.

"I worked on one for an officer. As a favor. It had a busted firing pin. Had to make a whole new one. Made it from scratch, out of tooled steel. See, it—"

Austin broke in. "And what's the name of the officer?"

Garfield's eyes went to Caldwell again. Did he have permission to talk?

That was it. Austin blew sky high. "Forget about him!" he raged. "Look at *me!*" Garfield, startled, looked at him. "The officer's name!" Austin hollered.

Garfield looked at Caldwell. Caldwell, impassive, nodded.

"Colonel Lawrence," Garfield said.

Austin was stunned. He couldn't believe it. For a minute he thought Caldwell with his oh-so-unsmiling face and this shit-eating topkick were making a horse's ass out of him with some stupid kind of joke. "Paul Lawrence?" he asked. Slowly, the light dawned. He turned to Caldwell. "You knew!" he exclaimed. "You knew! You goddamn knew, didn't you?"

Caldwell didn't crack a muscle. He kept his profile rocklike as he dismissed the sergeant. "That's all, Garfield."

The colonel spun on his heel and strode across the anteroom toward the door. Austin, forcing himself to calm down, followed him. Behind them, half-hidden by the Dutch door, Sergeant Garfield had the last word. "Did I say something I shouldn't?" he yelled. He was greeted by the slamming of the door.

"I don't believe it," Austin roared, hustling to keep up with Caldwell's long, purposeful strides as they burst out of the building and headed for the parking lot. "You're still trying to protect that asshole Lawrence!"

"Bullshit," the colonel answered coolly. "You're carrying a grudge."

"You goddamned officers make me sick!" Austin bellowed. "You already know that Lawrence is innocent, right? How do you figure that?"

Caldwell stopped at the curb. He reached in his jacket pocket for a cigar and started rolling it between his fingers to loosen the paper. All without taking his eyes off Austin. "In this country you're supposed to be innocent until proven guilty, boy," he said.

Nothing could have gotten Jay Austin madder. "Don't call me boy!" he yelled. "I'm no goddamned boy!"

Caldwell bit off a hunk of the cigar and reached for a match.

"Let's go talk to him," Austin said, biting back his temper.

Caldwell shook his head, puffing on the stogie to get it lit. "No way," he said around the stinker. He squinted against the sun and pinned Austin with his steely eyes. He had a crooked smile that was almost worse than his grimace. They stood there eyeing each other. Two roosters ready to peck each other to death over barnyard rights. Caldwell's cigar went out.

"I'll get a warrant," Austin said finally.

Caldwell's smile got broader, but not a hell of a

lot nicer. "See how far you get trying to serve it on a federal reservation," he said.

Again, a standoff. Austin's teeth were starting to ache. God, he'd love to take a poke at this superior, insufferable sonofamilitarybitch. And he knew Caldwell was feeling likewise. He turned away from the colonel and started across the lot toward his car. But Caldwell started talking, without moving a step. Austin stopped and listened.

"Since you got here, you've been trying to piss on me," Caldwell said. "Like I'm some tree in a park. That's because you didn't think you needed me for anything. Well, suddenly it's a little different."

Austin imagined—he hoped it was only his imagination—that little chips of tooth were being ground off inside his mouth. He tried to stop it but he was so damned mad and getting madder, he had to do something, and at least that was something that didn't show.

"You want to talk to Colonel Lawrence—or any other personnel on this base—you do it my way. You got me?" Caldwell ordered.

Austin burned and didn't trust himself to say anything. Caldwell went on talking. "What happened between you and Lawrence happened a long time ago," he said. "You were wrong then and you're wrong now. There's a proper way to do things. And, if you want to do anything with my help, you're going to do it the proper way."

That was more than he could stand. Austin spun on his heel and headed for the Dodge. He hauled open the door, looked back. Caldwell was still standing there, calmly relighting that goddamned cigar. "You coming?" Austin yelled.

Caldwell waved him on. "I'll walk."

Austin took off, leaving tracks smeared into the pavement. He came up with words between the

Presidio and the precinct house that he didn't even know he knew. Fat chance he'd have that dinner with Donna now—or ever. Smashing as she was, the poor girl would probably die an old maid and maybe even a virgin, with a warlord like Caldwell for a father.

Austin slogged home to figure out what he had and what he didn't have. His desk was an oasis of neat precision in the chaos of the apartment. It was not unlike the corner of his mind reserved for clear, concise, unemotional, reasoned thinking—the corner that made him a good inspector on his way to being even better. He walked into the apartment, kicked aside a stack of magazines and sat down at the oasis. In the next hour, he forgot about pert, pretty blondes and fire-eating provost marshals. He was in pursuit of a challenge, trying to decipher a puzzle that didn't make any sense—yet.

He took a sheet of ruled paper from a drawer on his right. It had blue lines to write on and a thin red line vertically down the middle. On one side of the ledger he began to list the known facts; on the other side, questions to be answered. At the top of the sheet he put the date; tomorrow's version would, he hoped, move the balance somewhat from Column B to Column A. By the time the case was finished, there would be all facts and no more questions.

In the FACTS column:

5:38 A.M. Patti Jean called in for ID on car license UDW 137: clean 1984 car.

PJ's last call-in was checking open door at club 5:42 A.M. Door found jimmied.

Patti Jean shot at close range in storeroom approximately 5:45 A.M.

Ballistics on bullets that killed PJ: Tokarev 33.

PJ's own gun, not fired, still in her hand.

Two trees in storeroom, one wet, one dry. Mueller says he didn't water. Mueller says nothing missing.

MP Meredith piled up chasing speeding '86 Lincoln southbound on Sheridan 5:52 A.M. MPs Sherman and Henry picked up Lincoln heading for Lombard Gate, it sideswiped them into wall approx. 5:54 A.M.

SF cops Schmidt and Dotson picked up Lincoln corner Lombard and Leavenworth 5:57 A.M., followed to Madison, Laguna, California. Requested Code 3 pursuit 6:08 A.M. Cruiser spun out at foot of Taylor, crashed into park, exploded approximately 6:15 A.M. Bullet found in Dotson's skull, probably fired from moving Lincoln.

Ballistics on bullet in Dotson's head: Tokarev 33.

Colonel Paul Lawrence owns Tokarev 33.

And in the QUERIES column:

Were these plates stolen (not reported) or did PJ misread?

Double-check anything missing from storeroom?

Significance of watered tree? Or dry one?

Who owns the Lincoln?

Need to know if Lawrence's gun is *IT*.

Need Caldwell to get info from army hardasses. There must be another way????

Who—

The phone rang. Austin put down the pen and got up, stretched and ambled over to pick it up.

"Austin here."

"Caldwell here."

It sure as hell wasn't the colonel. Her voice was as pert and tangy as her looks. Delicious.

"Well, hi," he said, softening like a lump of melted chocolate. He sank down in the armchair, cradling the phone against his shoulder.

"You didn't expect me to call," she said, more of a statement than a question.

"Well, sure, I did. I hoped you would, anyway. How about dinner?"

"How about it?"

"Tonight?" he asked.

"I'll ask my daddy," she teased.

Austin laughed. "You want to bring him along, as a chaperone?"

"Well, what a sweet idea! Yes, I just think I will! Thanks for suggesting it."

"Hey, you're not serious. Are you? Oh, God, tell me you're kidding. You're kidding, aren't you? Donna?"

She let him hang there for a minute and finally she answered, trying to sound stern and not making it. "You shouldn't make promises you don't intend to keep," she said.

"That wasn't a promise. That was a . . . a terrible suggestion."

"Oh, especially you shouldn't make suggestions you don't intend to follow up!"

"You're nice, Donna."

The sudden turnabout in tactics worked. The hint of a hard edge disappeared. "Nice, huh? Well," she said in a softer tone, "that remains to be seen."

"Do you know Molly Bloom's, that new place that opened a couple of months ago?" he asked her.

"Sure."

"Meet you there about seven?"

"Oh, you don't want to come to my house and

pick me up, maybe have a nice friendly chat with my father?"

"You're cute."

"So are you," she said, and hung up the phone.

It was hard to go back to thinking about murder and car chases and logical procedure after that. Anyway, he hadn't gotten much sleep the night before, what he remembered of it, and he was hoping not to get much tonight. So he stashed the facts-and-queries sheet in the top drawer and hit the sack. His last conscious thought was the hope that he'd dream about Donna without dreaming about her father.

CHAPTER 6

ALAN CALDWELL JOGGED around the periphery of the base, passing along West End and the Golden Gate Promenade around five in the afternoon, just as the thick white whipped-cream started rolling in under the bridge. He liked to time his run so that he'd get the full benefit of the best view in the world just at sunset, when the temperature dropped suddenly and cold air overtook the sluggish warmth of a California day. The resulting fog was silent, ominous, and beautiful. Alan Caldwell was a tough, sharp-eyed man with a reputation for driving himself as hard as he drove others. He wouldn't want it known that he jogged this way every evening for the view, although he was straight enough with himself to admit it, muse on it, and find himself the better man for it.

By the time he finished his ten miles and turned into the walkway leading to his house, it was completely dark and his breath was visible in the light from the lampposts. He meant to go upstairs and grab a cold shower, as he usually did, but a glance into the living room told him that Donna had a good fire going. His chair was in front of the fire, turned halfway to the fireplace and half to the television set, which was already tuned to the football game. He hesitated in the hall for a minute. "Fourth down and one yard to go," the announcer shouted, all thrills, and Caldwell decided the shower could wait.

A thorough-going sort of man, he had prepared the area before going out on his run. Now it looked irresistibly inviting. Next to his chair was a small round table on which sat a humidor filled with fat cigars, a box of old-fashioned kitchen matches, a deep ashtray and a manila folder with a neatly typed blue and red label:

PERSONNEL FILE
LAWRENCE, LT. COL. PAUL

He sat down and caught his breath. He stretched out his Reeboks to the warming fire. A glance at the television screen; the Rams were being rammed back to their own goal line. He selected a cigar, took a while to light it, then picked up the folder and started reading.

He glanced up to see Donna, looking winsome and too grown-up—damn, that happened fast! She was wearing a rather low-cut sweater that showed the shape of her breasts in a way he would have appreciated a lot more in any other woman in the world. Her skirt was made out of a smooth soft silk, the same color as the sweater. She was a knockout. She was carrying a coat over her shoulder.

"So who's winning?" she asked, gesturing at the TV.

Caldwell reached for the remote and muted the sound of the overexcited announcers and the cheering crowds. "I don't know. Bad guys, probably," he said. "You're not going out dressed like that, are you?" He said it casually, but he wasn't joking.

"Like what?" she teased. She went over and kissed him on the forehead. He wasn't going to skip it, though; he cared too much about her and he knew much too much about what men did to young women who looked like her. What a curse, to become the man who knew too much about the kind of man he used to be. To worry about the person you loved most in the world because the world was full of guys just like you were—scoring, hitting and missing, kissing and running, taking no woman seriously, but taking them all. Until he met the one he never wanted to run from, the one who gave him Donna and then died. A stitch of pain hit him, as it always did when he was forced to remember his loss. She looked like her mother, and it frightened him—him!—to think about the bad stuff that could happen to a beautiful young woman in this world.

He put on what he thought of as his "stern parent" look. He pointed to the short hem of her skirt. "Might as well not wear any skirt at all as wear that," he commented drily.

She laughed. "There's a thought," she said.

He didn't know what to say. He fought the impulse to drag her upstairs and lock her in her room. What an old fogy the young lion has become, after all. But I have to protect my cub, my girl, my darling daughter. I didn't like that smartass Austin hanging around here; what was he doing hanging around here? He could have caught me at the office. He had put the papers down and was staring at the soundless game: twenty-two huge bruisers dressed up like Buicks, ramming each other on a cold snowy field in front of thousands of silently raving maniacs. Every one of those guys was looking for a girl like Donna to maul.

"Okay," Donna was saying. "What's bothering you, old chum?"

He looked up at her. "You're seeing Austin, aren't you?"

Donna wasn't retreating from him; she was protecting her privacy, her right to live her own life. She was twenty-one and wouldn't be treated like a kid and he was glad she felt that way, only it made him crazy when she just answered: "Maybe."

"I don't think that's a good idea," he said in his most reasonable tone.

Donna surprised him with a grin. "He told me you'd say that," she said.

Caldwell turned his eyes back to the TV. Silence reigned. Donna pushed his arm off the chair and perched there, her arm around his neck.

"Oh, he did, did he?" Caldwell said, irritated but careful not to push her away. "Did he tell you why?"

"That's between you and him," Donna said. She laid her cheek lightly on the top of his head.

"Yes, it is," Caldwell agreed. "Okay? And you shouldn't get in the middle of it."

Donna got up. "I'm just going out for dinner. I don't tell you who to see."

"You're goddamn right you don't," Caldwell retorted.

"And if I did, I don't know if I would choose Myra—that's her name, isn't it? The redhead with the giant hermans who makes you breakfast every Thursday morning?"

Caldwell put the papers on top of the folder, face down. He stood up. "That's different," he told her. She looked quizzical: different how? Well, okay. He was going to have to spell it out. He had a moment's longing for the days when she was a little kid and anything he said was golden and true. He reached for her hand. "There are things you don't understand," he said. "Austin used to be an MP. He was posted here. I was his CO."

Donna nodded. "He told me that much."

"He told you a lot," Caldwell said.

She shrugged, but she didn't take her hand from his. "He told me some," she said.

"Don't be fooled by him," he told his girl. "He has no respect for women." This way to the Old Fogy's Hall of Fame. God, how could he explain to her; it *was* different, damn it.

"And you have enormous respect for Myra," Donna said sarcastically. Now she did pull her hand away. "I know I do," she added.

Sadly, Caldwell shook his head, tried another tack. "He'll use you to get at me," he warned her, knowing she wouldn't listen, knowing it was true.

"Are we going to fight again?" Donna asked sharply.

"I care what happens to you, goddamn it!" Caldwell pleaded. This was not one of the things he was good at. He was good at lots of things, but this was not one of them. Why the hell wasn't the kid's mother alive when she was needed so by both of them?

"I know you care what happens to me," Donna told him sadly. "Well, what is it with you and him?"

"Can't you just take my word for it?" her father pleaded.

"No."

"Okay. Well, one night, a couple of years ago, when you were away at school, he and Patti Jean Lynch were out on patrol—"

Donna interrupted. "The girl who was shot the other night?"

He nodded. Donna's face showed her sympathy. For the girl, for the girl's ex-partner. Shit. This was not the way to do it. But he went on with the story; if she wanted to know, she had every right. After all, Donna was in the middle, sort of, or might get to be if she kept it up with Austin.

"They pulled over Paul Lawrence," he went on. "He had had a little too much to drink. Words were exchanged. Austin blew up."

"What do you mean, 'blew up?'"

"He claimed Lawrence insulted Patti Jean. So he beat the hell out of him, dragged him into the MP station, and tossed him into the drunk tank."

"And of course you went right down, got your fellow officer and gentleman out of the tank and took him home."

Caldwell's chin went up a notch; so did an eyebrow. "Even if Lawrence did insult her, there's no way Austin could justify beating him up."

"That depends on the insult, doesn't it?" Donna asked thoughtfully. She knew as well as he did that a noncom could end up serving twenty-five years in Leavenworth for striking an officer, although it was different for MPs. Sometimes. What she was really wondering was whether Jay Austin and Patti Jean Lynch had been lovers. It sounded like it.

"He was way out of line!" her father shouted, exploding. "He was an MP, for Christ's sake! How the hell can you defend him—you don't even know him!"

"Was I defending him?"

"Stay away from him," Caldwell said angrily.

"I have a right to find out about him," she told him. She could be just as stubborn as he was; she came by it honestly.

"I don't want you to see him."

She stared at her father, who glared back. "Is that an order?" she asked calmly. She didn't feel calm but her voice didn't let her down.

"It is," Caldwell snapped.

"What about our agreement?"

He didn't answer. Stiff-necked, he took a full drag of the stogie and blew its foul smoke into the television set. Pom-pom girls were shaking their asses, and fans were blowing on their fingers. You could see their breath.

Donna nodded sadly. "He told me you'd break that, too," she said. She turned and picked up her coat from the arm of the chair where she'd thrown it. She headed for the door. "Don't wait up for me. I might be late," she said.

The door closed quietly behind her.

Caldwell was either going to bawl like a baby or swear like a tartar. He took the cigar out of his mouth and threw it with all his might into the fireplace. Now it would stink up the whole room.

"Shit on a stick!" he growled, and then, louder, in anguish, he told the television precisely what it could do and where it could go to do it.

Donna walked into the restaurant and looked all around for him, but he hadn't arrived yet. What if her dad was right, what if Jay Austin was a real heel, what if he stood her up—so all right, then she'd know. She had to find out for herself, that was all. Simple. No big deal. She wondered if it would be different with her father if he weren't so used to giving orders and being obeyed without question. Or if her mother had lived . . . No point in going around that one any more. She was on her own, and she liked it fine. Her father would just have to accept the fact that she was a woman who didn't take orders from anybody. Once he learned that, he'd probably like her better for it. She hoped.

The place was crowded. It was on the quiet side, though, not one of those ear-blasting joints where you had to be deaf if you hoped to digest your food,

and where conversation was a thing of the past.
This was subdued—lighting was dim, music was
Mozart and soft—diverting, pleasant, background
music. Good choice, Austin. So where are you, by
the way?

She was shown to a table near the window. She
decided that she'd have a glass of red wine and
watch the passing scene for fifteen—no, give him
twenty—minutes, then if he hadn't shown up she'd
leave. Or order dinner, depending on how she felt
when the time came. With her mind settled on this
scenario, she was almost surprised, and outra-
geously pleased, when Austin came through the
door. She liked the way he looked around, serious
blue eyes scanning the place and then crinkling
with a smile when he spotted her. He was wearing a
clean white shirt and a quiet tie, and his jacket was
open. A shock of shag-cut hair fell over his forehead; he tossed it back with two fingers as he came
over to her. She liked the way he looked at her. But
she was still upset about the hassle with her father,
and it must have shown on her face, because his
smile turned quizzical as he slid into the seat
opposite her.

"Hi," he said.

"Hi."

"Ah . . . you . . . ah, you look really pretty," he
said. That was an understatement, but something
had changed, and he felt unsure of his ground all of
a sudden. She seemed a lot less friendly now than
she had been when a total stranger had knocked on
her front door that morning. Something wrong; he
would have bet the ranch it was the old bastard. But
maybe it was just a passing thing. "Uh . . . am I
late?" he asked, giving her the old warm-up smile.

Donna looked at her watch. "Ten minutes," she
said.

"Ten minutes isn't late," he protested.

She shrugged. "In my house, after five minutes they send out a search party."

The waiter came alongside and Austin ordered Absolut on the rocks. "Another glass of wine?" he asked Donna. She shook her head. This one was still three-quarters full. When the waiter was gone, Austin leaned forward. "You look great," he told her honestly.

"Some people say I look like my father," she stated flatly.

Austin leaned back again. "Christ, what a thought. Does he know where you are, by the way?"

Donna nodded. "He knows," she said. She took a sip of wine. Austin picked up the menu and started to study it. Donna played with the stem of the wineglass. Finally she said, "I have a question and I'd like a straight answer, okay?"

The waiter brought Austin's drink. Setting the menu aside, Austin tasted it, set it down. "That's the only kind I've got," he told her.

"Why did you want to have dinner with me?" she asked.

Austin couldn't believe it. Didn't she know how desirable she was, how attractive? Did her question mean what it said, or was he missing some secret ingredient here? "Why do you think?" he countered.

"I'm not sure. My father says you're using me to get at him."

"Ah, I see. Well, what do you think?" Austin asked her.

Donna frowned. "I'm not sure," she admitted.

"Look, your father and I don't like each other. That's not exactly a secret." He waited, but she didn't say anything. She was waiting for a fuller explanation, so he told her all of it. "There was an incident . . . it was when I was an MP. I busted a colonel, name of Lawrence. He was a real sloppy drunk who thought it would be a neat idea to see if he could do some tight figure eights with his Oldsmobile at two in the morning. I threw him in the tank."

"Did you beat him up?" she asked quietly.

She was asking frankly and she really wanted to know. Austin laughed, one of those one-syllable laughs that sound more cynical than they are. "I told you your old man would give you a lot of garbage about me," he reminded her.

"You also told me to find out for myself," she said.

He swirled the ice in his glass. He didn't answer right away, so Donna asked again. "Did you beat him up?"

"He resisted arrest," Austin told her. "Then he started in on my partner, who was a woman."

Quietly, not pretending either concern or unconcern, Donna asked the question that had been on her mind for the last hour. "Were you involved with her?"

Austin looked up and straight into her eyes. "She was my partner," he said, by way of explaining a great many things. Donna nodded, because she did understand now. She knew about the kind of special relationship people have when their lives depend on each other; she had heard stories about the buddy system all her life. "Anyway," Austin went on, "the guy got way out of line. He took a swing at me, so I hit him."

"Were you out of line?" Donna asked.

"Depends on how you look at it."

"How do you look at it?" she persisted.

He thought about it, and then he said, "He deserved it."

"And then?"

"And then . . . the son of a bitch demanded they court-martial me."

She didn't say anything; neither did he for a minute. Then he went on. "So in marched the colonel, without a second's hesitation. He didn't want to know why. 'Why' isn't in his book. Just what, when, and how much. There was an officer involved, and that's all that counted. Certainly not my side of it, not my word for it . . . I was just one of his men. So you know what the colonel did? He backed Lawrence. Lawrence walked, and I lost one of my stripes. That was it. Over and Out. So I got out."

She studied him closely in the dim light of the restaurant. She didn't say anything. He didn't have a clue how she was taking all this. That little doubt was still in her eye; he wished it would go away.

"Listen," he said, "the reason I'm here is that I'm interested in you. Not your father. Him I can take or leave alone. But you . . . you I want."

She looked down into her wine, and a smile danced around her lips. His heart gave an extra beat. Suddenly she looked back up at him, and said, "Prove it."

"What?"

Donna smiled. "We can do this two ways, you know. We can sit here and talk for a couple of hours . . . and wonder what it would be like if we were alone . . . or . . . we could just cut to the chase."

The lady was full of surprises. Austin couldn't move or even react for a minute; he just looked at her. Then he stood up and so did she. He pulled some money out of his wallet to leave on the table. He didn't stop to count it.

CHAPTER 7

THEY STOOD IN front of the restaurant, deliberately not touching. The current between them was too strong for casual hand-holding. They didn't even look at each other, or have anything to say. The car jockey pulled up from the rear parking lot in a vintage '62 Corvette that shone with a recent waxing and didn't have a dent or a scratch. Austin's blue Dodge, in slightly more disreputable condition, pulled up right behind it.

Donna stepped forward to claim the Corvette. "Nice car," Austin said, holding the door for her. "Pull across the street and follow me, okay?" He started for the Dodge.

She rolled the window down. "Oh, no," she said, laughing. "You follow me!" Austin stopped in his tracks, wheeled around. She had already started her engine and was revving up.

"Hey, you don't know where you're going!" he shouted after her, but it was too late, she had taken off, tires peeling. Frowning, Austin jumped into his car and raced after her.

He had a hard time keeping the Corvette in his

sights. She wasn't speeding, exactly, just heading for hills that didn't let you guess what was on the other side, steep curves and the general up-and-down, in-and-out thrills of San Francisco streets. The combination of sexual anticipation and near collisions kept Austin on the edge. She wasn't kidding when she said "cut to the chase," he thought. But if he'd taken his eyes off the road and caught his face in the mirror, he'd have noticed he was loving it.

He took a hill in first gear and crested, spotted the Corvette stopped at a red light down below. In a minute, he was alongside. He rolled down his window and shouted. "What the hell are we doing?"

His answer was a wide and sensationally exciting grin, but no information to speak of. She blasted off when the light changed and disappeared with a quick left turn into Chinatown's bustling Grant Avenue. He was right behind her, but he knew he'd lose her in the tortuous puzzle of winding alleys and extra-narrow streets. Frantic, he flipped on the siren. People and cars tried to get out of his way as he swerved off in a shortcut, down a passage barely wide enough for a car. He thought he spotted her a couple of times, always a block or more ahead, but by the time he caught up she was around a corner and up another alleyway. The tangled streets were lined with pushcarts heaped with bok choy and onions and roasted ducks and silk blouses and dried fish and tourist toys, all lit with brash neon or dim festive lanterns; night was as busy as day here. Crowds of people were shopping and selling and hawking and gawking, slow to move aside for a mere Dodge with siren. Any car, even with siren, was given room grudgingly, and ranks of people immediately closed behind it. He lost sight of the

Corvette. It wasn't fun anymore; this was a lousy game. It was hopeless.

Austin pulled over to the curb and pounded the dash with his fist in frustration. What the hell was she up to? Propositioning him, knocking the wind out of him with the most endearing suggestion he'd ever heard, getting him all worked up and then leading him on a goddamned chase and deliberately losing him. Maybe being the offspring of a hotshot colonel made you beautiful but bad, real bad. He turned the siren off and maneuvered down Ross Street past a pawn shop, a house of birds, a couple of restaurants, and an antique dealer. He finally made his way to Jackson Street, where things widened out a bit, and then pulled into the traffic and headed for home, muttering under his breath terrible things about the whole Caldwell family and their ancestors.

He roared down the hill, slowing in front of his house. His headlights picked up a woman standing at the curb. The bright lamps saw right through the sheer skirt she wore; he could see a perfect outline of her legs, which were sensational. But that didn't make him any less mad at her. He crimped the wheels against the curb and came out fighting.

"Are you out of your mind?" he shouted.

But she just smiled and held up the little white card he'd given her with his home address scrawled across the back. Then she did something so strange and wonderful he forgot everything else. She grabbed him by the neck and kissed him so passionately he fell back onto the hood of her Corvette. It was still hot from the chase.

She was writhing on top of him, pinning him with her legs wrapped around his thighs, going to work on his tie and his shirt buttons. Weakly, he thought about the neighbors and the fact that it was only about eight o'clock at night and nobody would be sleeping yet. They'd all be at the windows or out walking their dogs and here he was getting raped right in front of his own house and nobody was going to do a damn thing about it. He tried to pull away. She was determined. She got his tie off, threw it in the direction of the street. He heard someone walk past, speaking Spanish in a lowered voice, but her kisses were covering his eyes and his mouth and his throat and he was damn near a goner. He heard his shirt buttons pop and she ripped it off him.

She was going to do it, too. As soon as he realized that, he found the strength to pull them both up off the hot metal. He picked her up and carried her across the street. His jacket fell on the sidewalk but they ignored it. She was kissing him and he was kissing her and somehow he carried her all the way into his building and over to the elevator. His buttonless shirt was hanging from one arm, probably in shreds. She was working on his belt when the elevator door opened, presenting an elderly couple on their way up from the basement laundry room. The man had a white mop of hair and a box of Tide in one hand, with the other he held hands with the elderly woman, who smiled sweetly at Austin.

Austin moaned. There was no way the two of them in their present state were going to get in that elevator with Mr. and Mrs. American Gothic. He spun around, headed for the stairs. Donna squirmed sensuously in his arms and ran her fingers down his spine and his chest while her tongue explored his mouth. He staggered up one flight, then another. Her sweater was abandoned on the first landing; his belt on the second. His knees were buckling.

By the time he made it to his own front door, his pants were down around his ankles. He was staggering. Where was the goddamned frigging lunatic *key,* for Christ's sake? Fuck it. He kicked the door so hard it exploded open. Chest heaving, mind reeling, body straining, he headed for the bedroom.

The anxiety of chasing her through the streets, dragging her up the goddamn stairs, and the absolute thrill of her untamed passion ignited a carnal rampage wilder than any he had ever known. He tore at her skirt and panties, crushing her beneath him. She hammered back, her eyes blazing. Together they rode a whirlwind, ultimately crashing to earth, breathless and sparkling.

Spent, he pulled a sheet over them, without releasing her from his arms. Their bodies touched each other all the way down to their toes. Nestled together against the pillows, they looked out at the necklace of lights down below on Fisherman's Wharf.

"I'm glad I didn't meet you before," he murmured. "If I'd known old Caldwell had a daughter like you, I might have re-upped."

She chuckled. "That would have been tragic." She traced the hairs on his chest with a gently teasing finger.

Austin sighed. Total exhaustion had never felt so good. "What did you do when you were away at school?" he asked idly.

"Are you going to ask me a lot of questions now?" she wanted to know.

"Well, I'm a cop. I can't help it." They lay quietly thinking that over. Then he said, "What are you going to be when you grow up, beautiful Donna?"

The quiet spell was broken; something had happened and they both felt it. She didn't move away physically, but still they were separating at the speed of light. When she answered him, the loving vulnerable softness was gone.

"I don't know," she said. "I'd like to teach, I guess. Dad doesn't think that's too swift an idea. He'd be happy if I married an officer and had a million kids." She stopped caressing his chest and lay perfectly still against him.

"Does he have the officer picked out already?" Austin asked. She didn't answer. "What about your mother?" he persisted. "She and your father divorced?"

Donna didn't answer for a long time. Then she moved away from him and sat up. He admired the line of her back and shoulders, her fine smooth skin, the way her hair fell. He waited for her to say whatever it was that seemed too difficult to get out. He wanted to hold her, but respected her moves. Finally, she said, "My mother killed herself when I was two. I never got to know her."

He was stunned. "Jesus," he said lamely. "I'm sorry."

She nodded her head once, and then she moved her incredible legs over the side and got out of bed. She started to dress, picking up her clothes where they had been tossed. Austin propped himself up on one elbow, watching her. He realized that he was hungry for her, and maybe it was a hunger that was going to take a long time to abate.

"I want to see you again," he said.

She picked up her skirt and put it on. She smiled at him. As she went out the bedroom door, she said, "I'll call you," and was gone. Austin fell back on the pillow, feeling her still wrapped in his arms. He stared out at the lights; they seemed clearer, more beautiful, than they ever had before, and Austin understood that he himself had changed. He had never met a woman remotely like Donna Caldwell; she was big trouble and all he wanted was more, more, more.

He slept like a bear in deep hibernation, and woke with the bright sunshine, feeling fine—which was a good thing, since he was about to take on the undefeated team of colonels: Caldwell and Lawrence. Bring on the two of them together, what the hell, he thought as he whipped through a bracing shower and climbed into his clothes (remembering his jacket getting tossed somewhere, wondering if he'd ever see it again, grinning to himself). I can tackle anything today. I wonder if she'll call me. And I wonder, if she doesn't, whether I'll call her. Absolutely yes. He took a look at the door, which was off its hinges. His jacket, neatly folded, had been placed on the carpet just outside his door. Abashed and grinning, he spent nearly an hour repairing the door. He never would know who had returned the jacket. Maybe it was true that all the world loves a lover.

All the way to the Presidio and winding along the drive to the officers' houses, he wondered if he would see her. But Caldwell was at the curb in front of his house, waiting. Military precision. Without a word, he got into the car. "Building 86," he said, instead of "good morning." Austin just nodded and headed over toward Crissy Field and the bay. It was a glorious day, a spanking new summer day, with cumulus clouds white and billowing against the clear expanse of bright blue sky. Austin felt like whistling, singing, at least turning the radio to a commercial band and listening to a little music. But he held himself in check and tried not to smile. Funny how one member of a family can make you feel so great and another member of the same family can frost your toes.

Building 86 was a two-story job built right after World War II, and kept in A-one condition by all the slave labor one finds on a military base. Austin turned into the lot and followed Caldwell into the building, taking a hop-skip to catch up to the colonel's long strides. The hallway was brown, polished and gleaming. There was wax on the floor about an inch deep. Lots of uniforms and some civilians behind desks, all looking busy, talking on the phone or to each other, typing and filing and shuffling papers in and out. Caldwell stopped at an open door where a sign read DIRECTOR OF PERSONNEL.

Caldwell turned to Austin before opening the door. "You take it easy," he said. "I'll do the talking." It sounded like an order, but for now Austin let it go by.

The door opened into a large square room with desks scattered around and a gang of employees and enlisted men all busily typing away on transfer orders and paychecks. On the right was a huge great oak door, carved and thick. The nameplate read: LT. COL. PAUL LAWRENCE. Just outside the door, an attractive secretary wearing oversized hornrims looked up and smiled at Caldwell. He smiled at her, too, and for a flash Austin saw what the colonel could do to the ladies: a crooked grin, a crinkling of the eyes, a frankly sexual appraisal. Caldwell deployed the message to the woman in question all in the blink of an eye; Austin realized he could take lessons from the bald old son of a bitch. But not for use with the colonel's daughter. Austin wondered if Caldwell knew how liberated his daughter really was. How uninhibited, how—he forced himself to think of other things, cold and impersonal, unpleasant things. Lt. Col. Paul Lawrence.

"Good morning, Colonel Caldwell," the secretary was saying. "Colonel Lawrence is waiting for you."

Caldwell glanced wryly at Austin as if to say,

"See? We're a minute and four seconds late and guess whose fault it is." But he didn't say a word, just opened the door to Lawrence's office. Austin frowned. His teeth started grinding again as he stepped inside, right behind Caldwell.

It was a nice office, especially for a military base. Large, with an imposing desk in the center. Two windows with brown venetian blinds overlooked the parade grounds. A brown leather couch took up most of the opposite wall. Lawrence was slouched in a huge leather swivel chair behind the oversized desk. He looked up with a smile on his face for Caldwell, but then he saw Austin and the smile was scuttled by a twitch that started jerking the muscles in his face.

"What's he doing here?" he snapped. He sat upright in the big executive chair, which looked much too big for him. Lawrence was a smallish, pinch-featured man with little eyes. What was left of his hair was mouse-colored. His mouth was pursed in a wrinkled little circle.

"Paul, there are a couple of questions . . ." Caldwell started to say, letting it trail off.

"What the hell is this?" Lawrence chirped. Austin just stood there letting the hate show on his face.

"I'm afraid this is official business," Caldwell told his fellow officer.

Austin couldn't keep quiet another millisecond. "Where's the gun, asshole?" he burst out.

Lawrence stared at him, then at Caldwell. "What?" he asked, sounding truly bewildered.

Caldwell's answer was merely to look sideways at Austin and say, with disgust, "You really are smooth."

Austin didn't take his eyes off Lawrence. "Where's the goddamned Tokarev?" he demanded.

73

Lawrence sneered. "Up yours, kid," he retorted.

Austin tensed; his whole body readied to make a move on the miserable son of a bitch. He felt Caldwell's restraining hand lightly settle on his shoulder, and he held back—but only barely.

"We need your gun," Caldwell told Lawrence, almost regretfully. "It's part of a homicide investigation. You have a Tokarev 33. We need to see it."

Lawrence stared at Austin's shoulder where Caldwell's hand still rested. "I don't have to answer any of this punk's questions," he snarled, "and I'm not going to."

Austin wanted to kick the shit out of him; the feeling was obviously mutual. Caldwell was the referee. "Listen to me, Paul," he said. "You're just prolonging the inevitable. He can get a federal judge."

"Let him," Lawrence snapped. "I don't give a damn. I will not submit—"

Caldwell interrupted. "I don't want it to come to that. Give me the gun. I'll check the slugs against those from the other night. When they don't match, you can have it back and this guy will be out of your hair forever."

Blustering, Lawrence got up from his easy chair and went over to the window. When he turned his back on them, Austin saw that it was visibly soaked from sweat. The sun was pouring into the room and it was a warm day, but not *that* warm. Interesting.

"I don't have it anymore," Lawrence said, out the window.

"Where is it?" Caldwell asked.

"I lost it in a poker game a couple of weeks ago."

"Who to?" Austin snapped.

Lawrence turned from the window. "None of your goddamned business," he told Austin.

"I'm making it my business."

74

"Get the hell out of my office. Now!"

Unexpectedly, Caldwell grabbed Austin's shoulder tightly, and turned him for the door. "Come on," he said.

"What, are you nuts?" Austin was furious. "I'm not going to—"

"Come on, I said!" Caldwell barked sharply.

Austin turned back to Lawrence, even as Caldwell was steering him, shoulder first, toward the door. "You can't stay on the Presidio forever," he hollered back at the sweating officer. "You gotta come out of your hole sooner or later. And when you do, I'll be waiting. You'll be on my turf and I'll own your ass. You understand?"

Austin shrugged himself out of Caldwell's grasp and left the room like he'd been shot out of a cannon. This time it was Caldwell who had to scurry to keep up.

CHAPTER 8

Austin's mouth was still working as they walked out of Building 86. "No way, you're not gonna pull that officer crap on me again. No way!"

"I'm impressed," Caldwell commented drily. "You handled that really professionally."

They reached the Dodge and Austin yanked the door open. Instead of getting in, he faced Caldwell across the roof of the car. "That jerk-off was lying," he said. "And if you keep trying to protect him, we're going to have serious problems."

Caldwell shook his head. "Tell me," he said, with no smile to soften the sarcasm, "what do you hear from your head lately? Even with one as empty as yours, an occasional thought sometimes manages to creep in." He opened the door on his side and got in. That left Austin staring at air, so he got into the car, too. Caldwell got out a cigar and started to unwrap it. Austin looked at him, waiting. "Maybe we don't need the gun," Caldwell explained, more slowly than he really needed to. "Maybe we already have a bullet." He busied himself with the matches and drawing on the cigar while waiting for Austin to catch up. "Careful," he said between puffs, "don't try too hard. You'll pull something."

Austin stared at him, the light dawning. Well, he'd never underestimated the brains of the colonel, it was his attitude that sucked. Caldwell had the stogie going; now he had Austin going, too. He threw the Dodge into gear and headed out for the rifle range.

Sergeant Garfield was inhaling coffee and testing whether it was possible to gobble a large sticky doughnut in three bites. Spotting Caldwell and Austin at the Dutch door, he jumped to his feet in a hailstorm of powdered sugar.

"At ease, Sergeant," Caldwell told him.

"Yessir."

"First swallow the doughnut and then see if you can answer my question. When you fixed the firing pin on Colonel Lawrence's Tokarev, did you test it to see if it worked?"

Garfield gulped the whole thing down in one disgusting swallow. "Yes, sir," he answered, blowing sugar flakes. "I capped it four or five times, Colonel."

Austin couldn't keep his mouth shut. "Any chance you still have one of the slugs?" he asked impatiently.

Garfield pointed to an oversized water barrel on the far side of the room that was used to test-fire weapons. Caldwell unlatched the lower half of the door and the two of them strode over to the barrel, the sergeant right behind them. The water came to within six inches of the top of the barrel. A coat hanger was hooked over the side of the barrel; Garfield took hold of it, reached down into the water with the hook and came up with a piece of wire mesh. As the water dripped off it, Austin and

Caldwell could see a mountain of bullets caught in the mesh. Garfield ran his hand across the knobby surface.

"Should be easy to spot," he said. "Tokarev's only a 7.62 millimeter. It'll stick out like a sore thumb with these 45s and 9s."

They all spotted it at the same time. At the bottom of the mesh there was a bullet smaller than the rest. Garfield reached for it, pushed it out of the netting and handed it to Caldwell. "Here's one, sir. This one came from the Tokarev."

"Lawrence's Tokarev," Austin commented, just making absolutely sure.

"Colonel Lawrence's Tokarev," the sergeant reiterated, after eyeing his CO and getting tacit permission to speak. This alone was calculated to drive Austin bananas, but he held it in.

Caldwell held out his hand and Garfield laid the bullet in it. Then there were some papers to sign in quadruplicate and finally they were out of there. Austin wanted that bullet a whole lot. Out on the grass, Caldwell said, "If this matches the slugs taken out of my MP and your cop, I want your word that you will go through me." He fixed Austin with his steely eyes.

"Sure," Austin said, reaching for it.

Caldwell closed his fingers over the bullet. "There's more," he said. "If this doesn't match, I want you to get off Lawrence's back and stay off it."

Austin looked Caldwell in the eye. He opened his mouth to say something, but Caldwell stepped in first. "Take it or leave it." Austin thought about it for a minute, decided the colonel meant exactly what he was saying, and could enforce it. And would. Anyway, he wouldn't need Lawrence if it turned out to be some other Tokarev, and he'd be just as happy to let the acquaintance drop.

"Deal," he said. He held out his hand. Caldwell dropped the bullet into his palm.

Austin pocketed the slug. He checked his watch. "Some guy named Peale reported his Lincoln stolen yesterday morning," he told Caldwell.

The colonel's eyebrows lifted; his face was all at attention. "He's a tough guy to see," Austin went on. "We're talking heavy money."

"So?"

Austin got to the point. "Well, I'm not going to ask you to come along. I'm not even sure I'd like it if you did."

Caldwell just kept looking at him, waiting.

"Well, if you want, it's okay. I guess. I got an appointment for two P.M." Austin hoped the brass would be having one of their military games or something, anything to keep Caldwell occupied elsewhere and let the police get on with their work. He waited uneasily for Caldwell's answer to his half-assed invitation, issued because it was required protocol.

"An appointment?" Caldwell mocked. "You're all charm and grace, boy," Caldwell said. He looked off at the blue sky and the bay where sailboats dotted the water like tiny triangular clouds dancing in the wind. "Pick me up at the museum," he said, and strode off without looking back.

Austin hit Park Presidio Boulevard and made for the ballistics lab. Caldwell strolled back to his office, taking salutes all along the way, his mind engaged in a puzzle starring a bright, quick-triggered, trouble-making cop who needed to be kept under tight control.

The Presidio Museum is housed in a two-story mansion that was built when Queen Victoria was still alive and giving her name to social inhibitions

79

and gingerbread architecture. The building sits stolid and imperial on its neatly trimmed lawn a couple of blocks east of the MP station. Its rooms and halls are now filled with military artifacts, historical moments caught under glass, indicators of time and events that won't stand still—except fleetingly, in museums such as this.

Over the main door, Caldwell read the banner announcing the current special exhibit: THE FLAGS OF WAR. A yellow school bus was parked in front of the building. The driver was leaning on one of the front fenders, catching some sunshine, glancing through a sports magazine.

The main gallery, an enormous space unto itself, had once been the entrance foyer. Its high ceilings (they didn't bother trying to heat it in the old days) currently supported flags, banners and guidons, each representing a piece of history. Glass cases along the walls and on the staircase landings held other flags, some too battle-tattered to hang any more, others too precious to leave to the ravages of twentieth-century air. Other military relics—swords, written orders, autographs, medals, bibles with browning edges once carried into battle by heroes, and scores of faded photographs—also sat in glass cases with little identifying notes.

Caldwell went over to the flag that had been raised on Mount Suribachi in Iwo Jima during World War II, made famous by a photographer who caught the exact moment when the Marines planted it. In the next case, battle flags shredded by enemy fire in Hue, Vietnam, Korea, World War I, the Spanish-American War, the Civil War, the original American Revolution—all were represented in this place.

In front of a Civil War display of blue and gray uniforms, a group of chattering, excited third-graders stood pushing their little noses as close as they could get to the glass. A slim young woman in skirt and sweater, obviously their teacher, kept an eye on them as they listened to a gruff-voiced but smiling white-haired man in civilian clothes telling them all about it.

"More American soldiers got killed in the Civil War than any other one," Ross Maclure, Sergeant Major (Retired), told them solemnly. He was wearing a bright polyester sports coat and a flowered tie. For twenty-five years in the army he hadn't had to think of what to wear, and his civilian taste was still forming. He'd only been retired a couple of decades or so. In his sixties, Maclure hadn't lost his physique. He worked out every day of his life. He took pride in being curator of the museum, keeper of the flame, and woe to anyone who belittled his job, his retirement, or, for that matter, his polyester civvies. His was a very important duty, and he was determined to do it right.

A little boy with bright eyes, in jeans and a T-shirt that proclaimed he had been to the Exploratorium spoke up. "How come more Americans got killed in that old war than all the others?" He looked up at Maclure, and the other kids waited for an answer too.

"Well, I'm glad you asked me that. What's your name, kid?"

"Julius," the little boy answered promptly.

"Well, Julius, it was because all the soldiers on both sides were Americans. Think about that."

Julius sized up the ex-top sergeant. "That's kind of lame," he decreed. He turned and wandered off toward another display.

Maclure didn't miss a beat. Thirty years in the Army and you knew how to handle hotheads. He turned back to the Civil War case. "This flag was flying at Fort Sumpter in 1861, when the war started," he told them.

Across the room, Julius had found something interesting. In one of the glass cases, a soldier mannequin was wearing a World War II Army uniform. On the sleeve were the six stripes of a First Sergeant. On the chest was an impressive array of campaign ribbons and decorations. Draped around the neck was a medal hung on a light blue ribbon with white stars. The medal was suspended from a bronze bar on which was imprinted a single word: VALOR.

"Hey, what's this stuff?" Julius sang out. Immediately, several of the children deserted Maclure and scurried over to see. Julius was clearly leadership material.

"Never mind that now, Julius," Maclure said. "Come back over here."

A tall man in an officer's uniform suddenly stepped out from the shadowy entranceway. He lifted his voice to carry across the empty vaulted chamber. "Hey, Julius," he said, "get him to tell you what it is."

Maclure turned sharply; so did the teacher and the kids, all staring at this tall man with the silver oak-leaf cluster on his collar. He had a trim mustache and when he took his cap off his head was mostly bald. His eyes were laughing but his mouth wasn't. Maclure's face turned beet red.

"Don't listen to him," he said, flustered. "He's mentally incompetent."

The attractive young teacher glanced with more than a little surprise back at Maclure, wondering if this was going to be of more than passing—or educational—interest. She looked back at the colonel and waited as expectantly as the children.

"That's the Congressional Medal of Honor in there," Caldwell pointed out. "The highest medal any soldier can ever get."

The white-haired man was livid. "Who let you in here?" he fumed. Then he looked down at the kids' faces, all gawking at the officer. "Did you let him in here?" he asked in mock outrage. A couple of the girls giggled nervously.

The colonel ignored him. "Julius," he said, "take a close look at that photograph in there."

The little boy peered closely into the case. There was a photo of two men shaking hands. He pressed his nose against the glass and studied it.

From across the room, the colonel explained: "The man on the left is Lyndon Johnson. He was President of the United States. The soldier with him won the medal."

Maclure was practically foaming. "Don't they have any kind of security here?" he raged, but it was a benevolent, if exasperated, anger. "Just anybody can fall in off the streets?"

The other children pressed around Julius, staring at the medal, the photograph, and back at the colonel, waiting for more explaining.

"Does that soldier look familiar?" Caldwell asked them.

The kids studied it intently. Julius looked over at Maclure suspiciously.

"Remember, this was a long time ago. He wasn't nearly as ugly then," Caldwell said by way of a broad hint.

Little Julius put it together. "Holy shit," he whispered, reverently. The other kids, one by one, caught on, too.

"This relic of a man before you is Sergeant Major Ross Maclure. He's retired now, which is why he wears such funny clothes. Why don't you ask him how he won the Medal of Honor?"

Julius was about to ask. Maclure cut him off. "How old are you?" he asked gruffly.

"Eight," the boy told him.

"You want to live to be nine?" Maclure growled.

Caldwell laughed. "He obviously didn't win it for charm. It was in Vietnam. He was separated from his unit in the jungle, when he found a wounded officer who was pretty close to dead." Maclure studied his shoes. "He picked up the officer and carried him toward what he hoped were the American lines, but he came across the enemy."

Button eyes jumped from Caldwell to Maclure and back again. Little spots of steam appeared on the glass case as some of the kids pressed their noses closer to the Medal and the photograph. It was utterly silent except for Caldwell's voice; even the teacher was spellbound.

"They were ready to ambush an American patrol. So he put the officer down, and, with one M-16 and some hand grenades, he attacked. He was one against forty or fifty."

"Forty or fifty?" echoed Julius, so impressed he didn't know whether to believe it or not.

"Yes," Caldwell assured him. "And he wiped them all out—all of them—despite being wounded himself. Then he went back, picked up the wounded officer again and carried him to safety."

The great hall was absolutely silent. And then bright-eyed Julius spoke up again. "What's that gun?" he said, pointing inside the case to a pearl-handled revolver.

"That's a forty-five the wounded officer gave him as a kind of present, a gesture for saving his life."

Another child spoke up, a little girl with brown pigtails tied in red ribbons. "What's Vietnam?" she asked.

Caldwell didn't know what to say. He glanced over at Maclure. Neither did he. The children's teacher came to the rescue.

"It's a place, Lily. A place where we fought a war."

"I never heard of it," the child said shyly. A few of the others murmured their agreement.

"Well, it happened," the teacher said.

They thought about this. One boy said he had heard of it before. Then Julius, spokesperson for the bright majority, asked the key question. "Did we kick ass?"

His teacher spoke up quickly. "I want you all to thank the sergeant major for taking the time to give us this tour."

The class chimed, "Thank you, Sergeant Major" in unison.

"You guys come back any time," Maclure told them.

The teacher ushered her class off to the restrooms before the bus trip back to school. As they disappeared around the corner, Julius's insistent question could be heard again: "Did we kick ass?"

Caldwell walked over to the Civil War display where Maclure was still standing. "Thanks a lot," Maclure told him sarcastically.

"Don't mention it." Caldwell waved his hand as though the praise was more than he could bear.

Maclure turned to head through the hall into a series of rooms that opened off each other. "I should have left your worthless Scotch ass in that jungle," he muttered.

"Scotch is a drink," Caldwell explained wearily. They'd been through this before, a couple of hundred times. "A man born in Scotland is a Scotsman."

Maclure looked at him in fond disgust. "Next time you're dying in the boonies," he said, "call a freaking cab, will you?"

They entered a smaller room that held more

souvenirs of the second world war. Maclure held the door for Caldwell and got a good close look at his face. When the door closed behind them, he dropped the phony anger and asked, with gentle concern, "Still worried about Donna?"

"I can't seem to have a conversation with her without one of us blowing our top," Caldwell confessed.

Maclure shook his big head. "She's not a little girl anymore, in case you haven't noticed. Maybe you don't want her to grow up."

Caldwell sighed and jammed his hands deep in his pockets. He rocked on his heels. "She's going out with Jay Austin. That name ring a bell with you?"

Maclure thought for a minute. "Oh, yeah, the young MP who tossed Paul Lawrence in the pokey, right?"

"Yes."

"I never liked Lawrence," Maclure said. "He's a monkey dick."

"You're a big help."

"Don't mention it."

"Austin's a cop now, SFPD. The female MP who was killed the other night was with him when he busted Lawrence three years ago. The thought of bringing Lawrence down after all this time is giving Austin a real hard-on."

"He's chasing the geek who shot his cop—has something to do with the MP's killing, is that it? And Lawrence is involved?"

Caldwell shrugged. "Don't know. The weapon that was used was a Tokarev 33. Lawrence has one—except he claims he lost his in a poker game."

Maclure looked at him keenly. "Did he?"

"I don't know. Austin doesn't think so. But—I don't know."

"So maybe Austin's right."

"Whatever it is, I know one goddamned thing, I don't want my daughter seeing him."

"Well, that ain't up to you, is it?" Maclure started walking slowly past the display cases of uniforms, battle helmets, insignia, canteens, medals and guns. Caldwell fell in alongside him and they paced the room.

"The only reason she's seeing him is because she knows I don't want her to," Caldwell said miserably.

Maclure grunted. "If that's true, then tell her you like him. Maybe she'll stop."

Caldwell stared at a bazooka placed on a pedestal like a piece of sculpture. "He's wrong for her," he said glumly.

"Maybe you're prejudiced."

"Maybe I know something about him—lots of things—that she doesn't."

"So tell her. Except—would *you* listen if someone told you not to see somebody?"

"That's different," Caldwell protested.

Maclure, from his vantage point of advanced age, nodded. "Sure. Sure it is."

They had circled the room but kept on going, strolling in step. They passed a case of Nazi artifacts, and another nearby load of souvenirs from Japan.

"Maybe you see a little bit of yourself in him," Maclure suggested.

Caldwell almost exploded. "What the hell do you mean by that?"

Maclure stopped, leaned against a glass case, and looked at Caldwell with a half-smile. "I mean I remember seeing this ninety-day wonder with a manual of orders in his pocket and I said to myself, 'Well, the Army finally found a way to screw me.'

But you didn't turn out so bad." He stopped and thought for a minute, and then he added, "It took a little time, though."

Caldwell smiled wryly.

"Maybe Austin just needs a little time," Maclure suggested.

Someone knocked on the door and opened it. "Anybody home?" It was Austin, looking to keep their appointment.

"Over here," Maclure said, gesturing to Austin to join them.

"Hey, Top, how're you doing?" Austin greeted Maclure.

"Still kicking. You still got a big mouth?"

Austin grinned. "Guess so."

"Figured," said Maclure. He turned to Caldwell. "Just a little time," he repeated, and left them to each other.

CHAPTER 9

O<small>NLY A COUPLE</small> of dozen blocks from the bucolic acres of the Presidio, up and down a few hills, the business district of San Francisco is snarled with traffic, honking horns, the smells of diesel oil and the occasional whiff of a roasted pretzel through the smog and soot. 731 Kearney Street is a sixteen-story office building in the heart of downtown. Austin pulled up in front of the building between a NO PARKING AT ANY TIME sign and a hydrant. He pulled a "Police Department Official Business" card from the glove compartment and stuck it on the dash. He and Caldwell got out and went into the building.

Gleaming marble, thick glass, and shining steel made the lobby into a setting for a space movie. The place was crowded with busy people in stylishly conservative suits and ties, skirts and low-heeled pumps, all either hurrying in, hurrying out, or hanging there waiting for the elevator. Caldwell and Austin joined the waiting group, and very quickly the elevator arrived. They got in and Austin reached for the diode "16," which glowed when it felt the approaching warmth of his finger.

The silent doors opened at the sixteenth floor. Thick red carpet stretched to meet them. A discreet set of names and numbers on the wall led them to a right turn, down a wide hall hung with original oil paintings, all professionally spotlighted. They stopped at a door marked Suite 1612: TRANSCORP. Austin opened the door and Caldwell, a bit off his turf, followed him in.

It was all soft grays and maroons. A table made out of a huge chunk of polished gray slate held an art book almost the same size. A receptionist sat behind a desk facing the door; five-six or seven, straight black hair down to her shoulders, frank black eyes, a pretty smile, and a plain gold wedding ring. She smiled pleasantly at them.

"I'm Inspector Austin. I phoned earlier. I believe Mr. Peale is expecting me?"

"Yes, Inspector. Just a moment, please." She called in and relayed his name, then hung up the intercom and flashed him her nice smile again. "Mr. Peale will see you now." She got up and the rest of her matched the smile. They followed her through a slate-colored glass doorway about three inches thick. They went down a wide, heavily carpeted hall to another door, which she opened and stepped back for them to enter.

Two glass walls leaned out onto the San Francisco skyline. It was a breathtaking view—both bridges, the bay, and Sausalito just behind Alcatraz and just before the mountains. On the other side of the room, about a mile and a half of black Italian leather couches formed a three-sided square around a huge, thick glass table with a telephone plugged into it.

The main feature of the grand-ballroom-sized

office was an ultramodern granite and glass desk, behind which sat a man in his forties, well barbered and manicured. Austin and Caldwell had a chance to observe him in action as he completed a phone call before turning to them. Square jaw, dark hair, slacks and jacket, about five-ten and 40 regular. At the side of the desk, with a gold-plated pen poised to take notes on a legal pad, sat a very young man, apparently an aide.

The receptionist waited respectfully until the boss said good-bye and hung up his phone. Then as he looked up at them, she said, "This is Inspector Austin, Mr. Peale."

"Thank you, Jane," Peale said, and the receptionist backed out of their presence, shutting the door silently behind her.

Peale looked at them, smiling and expectant.

"I'm Jay Austin, San Francisco Police Department, and this is Colonel Caldwell, the provost marshal of the Presidio," Austin explained.

Peale came around the slab of granite and motioned to them to approach. He held out his hand. "Hi. Arthur Peale," he said. "You guys want anything? Espresso? Beer?" He was genial, a regular guy.

"No, thanks," Austin said.

"This is Mark Wallach," Peale said, nodding toward the yuppie, "my assistant."

"Pleasure," Mark Wallach said, smiling and, Austin thought, almost bowing in his accustomed role of ass-kisser.

"Coffee for me," Peale told Wallach, who went over to the bar and started to make espresso-machine noises.

Austin sat down in one of the leather chairs drawn up before the desk. Caldwell remained standing.

"Now, how can I help?" Peale asked them. He went around and sat back down at his monster desk.

"I'd like to ask you a couple of questions, if you don't mind," Austin said.

The tycoon nodded, friendly, friendly, friendly. "Sure, no problem. I assume it's about my car you located."

"Your Lincoln was used in a homicide at approximately five-forty-five Tuesday morning at the Presidio," Austin told him.

Peale raised his pale eyebrows. "The one on the front page of the *Chronicle?*" he asked.

Austin nodded, the very polite and sympathetic cop. "I'm afraid so," he said.

Caldwell was restless on his feet. He had been quietly pacing the office during the entire conversation. As Mark Wallach came from the bar with a tray balancing a small coffee pot, cup, saucer, and lemon peel, Caldwell sauntered over to the bar. His keen eyes checked out the area.

Wallach put the tray down in front of his boss. "Did you hear that, Mark?" Peale said with a trace of excitement in his voice. "The Lincoln was involved in a shooting at the Presidio."

Austin watched Mark Wallach shake his head in horror; then he took a respectful step back while his boss sipped at the coffee.

"When did you last use the car, Mr. Peale?" Austin asked.

Peale put the little cup down. "It's my wife's car, Inspector. She dropped by Monday night and I took her to dinner. She parked in the lot that adjoins the building. It's not attended at night, of course, but it's always been perfectly safe before. It was late when we finished dinner, so we left her car there and drove home in mine. The next morning, the Lincoln was gone."

Caldwell spoke up for the first time. "What's Transcorp?" he asked abruptly, turning from the bar.

"We're a holding company. Fairly diversified at the moment," Peale told him. "We have a chain of jewelry stores, some shopping centers, a—"

Caldwell interrupted him. "Which restaurant did you and your wife eat in Monday night?"

Austin was annoyed. Peale was a civilian and not suspected of anything. It had been drummed into his own impatient head enough times that cops should be nice to the citizens they're trying to protect. And here came old Military Might charging at the guy as if he were a recruit with an untidy bed. No finesse, no tact, screwing up a perfectly amenable Q&A with trigger-happy snarls and questions that sounded accusatory. Austin shot him a dirty look, but Caldwell's piercing eyes were riveted on the rich man behind the desk.

"We ate at Jake's," Peale told him. He sounded cool enough, but Austin would have bet a bundle he was getting his back up. "It's a seafood place on Broadway," Peale explained, in case the colonel had never been off the base before.

"How far from your office—" Caldwell started to ask, but Austin had had enough. He stood up and cut in.

"Thanks a lot for your time, Mr. Peale," he said. "Your wife's car is at the Fourth Street garage. It's being printed and processed now. We ought to be able to get it back to her within ninety days. It's going to need a little dent work, I'm afraid, but I'm sure your insurance will take care of that."

Peale nodded. "Forget the car. I just hope you catch whoever shot those people."

Caldwell frowned and his mustache went stiff, but Austin headed for the door, held it open for him, and the colonel complied.

The minute they got out of the teeming lobby, Caldwell exploded. "Why were you in such a hurry to get out of there? Are you late for an appointment with your hairdresser?" he fumed.

"Hey," Austin pointed out, "you're the one who's real big on jurisdictions. Well, this happens to be *my* jurisdiction. I was conducting the goddamn investigation."

"You call that an investigation?" Caldwell shouted. There was a five-second pause while they got into the car. Then he simpered, pursing his lips so that his mustache almost formed a circle, " 'Ooo, I'm sorry to trouble you, Mr. Peale . . . sir . . . it's just that your car was used in a homicide . . . and . . . gee whiz, Mr. Peale . . . we're really sorry.' "

Austin started the engine with a fierce twist of the key. The motor turned over with a wrenching sound like barely controlled anger. "Colonel," he said between clenched teeth, "I don't know if you can handle this. This may be real hard for you to understand. But I have to break it to you, *sir*. You are *not* in command here."

Caldwell nodded. Austin let off the brake and slid into the traffic. They didn't say anything for a minute or two.

Staring straight ahead, Caldwell said easily, "You were in such a rush to get out of there. Did you happen to notice what he had on his bar?"

"I ran a make on Peale," Austin told him. "I put him through R&I a hundred times. I ran him up, down, and sideways. I don't like him, but he's clean."

Caldwell nodded. "When are you getting the ballistics report on the Tokarev slug?"

"In a couple of hours," Austin told him. He couldn't help wondering what Caldwell had found on the guy's bar, but there was no way he was going to ask.

"Well, we've got time for a cup of coffee," Caldwell said. "Come on, I'll buy you a cup."

Austin glanced over at him. "Are you kidding?"

"I'm not kidding," Caldwell said.

Driving east on Market Street, Austin spotted the Old Ferry Building looming ahead, and figured what the hell. He swung left onto the Embarcadero and pulled in at an oyster bar teetering on the edge of the bay. He parked in the lot and they stepped onto the pier and went inside. Music blasted from a jukebox, sawdust was sprinkled on the floor, and there were at least three levels of tables going up, all glassed in with views of the ferries, docked ships, and a helicopter landing pad from which tourists could circle Alcatraz. They sat down at a long counter. Down at the far end, a man in a soiled white apron was opening oysters. The place was relatively crowded, considering that it was mid-afternoon.

They ordered coffee. Nothing fancy, just caffeine in a mug. It tasted good, better than that bitter stuff Peale drank. Austin was in no hurry; he blew away the steam, sipped the brew, and waited to find out how come Caldwell was picking up the tab. He thought he knew.

He was right. "I want to talk to you about Donna," Caldwell said.

Austin grinned. "Are you going to ask me my intentions?"

"That's exactly what I'm going to do," Caldwell said sternly. He was staring straight ahead.

Austin laughed and blew on his coffee. "You're some piece of work, Colonel," he said. He shook his head and laughed again.

"What the hell's so funny?" Caldwell demanded.

There was an echoing laugh behind them, and then it got suddenly louder and then it was right in their faces. A huge slob in a red-and-black checked flannel shirt ambled up to the counter, his mean eyes all over Caldwell's uniform. The man's mustache trailed down the sides of his fat cheeks in a sad, inverted "U" that went all the way to his double chin. He was a monster.

"Hey, Major, how's it hanging?" the slob asked in a voice like an oinker rotting around in wet slops. He was looking for a brawl, mad at the Army, dying to flatten some brass. He thought his own remark the wittiest thing he'd heard since leaving the sty, and looked back to his playmates in a booth nearby for applause. They yukked it up and cheered him on.

"Eh, way to go, Dwayne."

"Make 'im sweat, Dwayne, boy!"

"Want to go?" Austin asked Caldwell quietly.

Caldwell kept his eyes straight ahead. He lifted the cup to his mouth and said, "After I finish my coffee." He took a calm, slow sip.

"C'mon, Major. I'm talking to you," Dwayne grunted, moving in closer.

"Let it alone, boy," Caldwell ordered.

"Oh, 'scuse me, Major. So sorry!" Dwayne mocked drunkenly.

Caldwell turned on his stool and looked Dwayne straight in the bloodshot eye. "I said let it alone," he repeated politely.

Dwayne turned back to his buddies and told them loudly, "Hey, did I hear him right? Did the Major give me an *order?*"

More laughter. Dwayne's friends crawled out of the booth like scorpions surrounding their prey. Austin turned to face them. He made them carefully, one at a time, just eyeballing them, waiting and ready.

With encouragement from his pals, Dwayne was unstoppable. He wrinkled his nose and came closer to Caldwell, put his snout right up against the uniform jacket and sniffed. "You stink, Major," he proclaimed loudly. "What the hell is that smell, anyway? Mothballs?"

His buddies loved that. They guffawed and snorted, pressing in a little closer. Caldwell looked at Austin, a silent signal: don't worry, I can take care of it. Dwayne reached over and put his cigarette out in Caldwell's coffee.

"What are you gonna do now, Major?" he prodded. The hair around his mouth and chin twitched with excitement.

"I'm not going to fight you, boy. I'm just going to use my thumb," Caldwell told him. His Brit accent seemed to get a little stiffer, a little more pronounced, when the adrenalin flowed, Austin noted. Austin's right hand set his coffee down and rested, ready, on the counter only inches from the holster slung under his left armpit.

"Your thumb? Your thumb, man?" Dwayne thought that was the funniest thing yet. Spittle flew from his lips as he sneered right up against Caldwell's face.

"My right thumb," Caldwell said. "Left one is too powerful for you."

That was it. Dwayne swung. Caldwell, ready, ducked it and stepped out from the counter, stabbing his assailant in the chest with his thumb. Dwayne staggered back, losing it for a second. His friends moved in closer.

Austin slipped his hand inside his jacket, came out with his 9mm, made sure all the boys saw it. "Keep it fair, guys," he said, with a hint of a smile. No argument. They backed off. He put it back in the holster.

Dwayne recovered his breath and snarled up at Caldwell. The colonel smiled and showed him the

thumb, pointed up. Dwayne bellowed and charged
—two hundred forty pounds of asshole intent on
bodily harm. Caldwell stepped aside. As he moved,
he jabbed the thumb deep into Dwayne's kidney.
The momentum shoved Dwayne backward into a
couple of winos having their midday pick-me-up at
the bar. They lost their footing, quickly recovered,
and removed themselves to the far end, out of
harm's way.

Dazed, Dwayne climbed to his feet. He looked at
his pals, who had stopped laughing. They weren't
about to get into this. Dwayne looked over at
Caldwell. He was smiling benignly, his thumb still
up.

The battle was bizarre and mostly Dwayne's—he
hit everything in the room except Caldwell. Walls,
chairs, tables were demolished. Every time he came
close enough, Caldwell ducked and jabbed with the
old thumb trick. Dwayne was getting crazy from
frustration, not to mention blows about the head
from the furniture he kept crashing into.

The manager of the place came over in a fury,
but when he saw Caldwell's brass he calmed down
and started enjoying the fight. After all, he had
insurance.

Austin noticed that Dwayne's pals were changing
their allegiance, cheering every time Caldwell's
thumb scored another victory. Anybody who could
take their best meatball with one thumb had to be
something good. Finally exhausted, unsure of
which end was up, Dwayne grabbed onto the
counter to steady himself and leaned in on Caldwell as if he were going to spit or say something or
both. Instead, Caldwell moved on him, pressing the
thumb against a spot on the thick red neck. Dwayne
slid to the floor. Caldwell leaned over him.

"See these little oak leaves, Dwayne? They're

silver. That means I'm a lieutenant colonel. If they were gold, that would mean I was a major. Understand?"

From his vantage point on the sawdust, Dwayne nodded and tried to speak. His voice came out all hoarse and cracked. "I think so," he said.

"That's good," Caldwell told him. "The next time you see an officer of the United States Army, you'll be able to recognize his rank. Then he won't get pissed off and accidentally hurt you." As if it were only an afterthought, he reached down with his right hand and dealt Dwayne one last, lasting thumb-jab on the carotid. The slob went out cold.

Caldwell dropped a dollar bill on the counter and headed for the door, with Austin behind him.

"About your daughter, sir," he said as he moved up quickly to push the door open for the colonel, "I'd like you to know, my intentions are strictly honorable."

CHAPTER 10

ALL WAS SILENCE except for the flutter of the red, white, and blue flag snapping in the breeze. A thousand men in Class A Greens, O.D. pistol belts, and spit-polished boots stood in salute to the star-spangled banner. The anthem began with the full-throated harmony of a fine military band; the proud music floated out across the greensward to the blue bay and the bluer ocean and the bluest cobalt sky overhead.

On the reviewing stand, the post commander stood at attention, with officers and dignitaries two steps behind him. At the head of the battalion, a lone officer held the salute. The last strains of the anthem drifted off into the crisp silence of the morning. The post commander terminated the salute and turned from the flag to face the troops.

"Bring your units to Order Arms!" he commanded.

Dropping his salute, the provost marshal spun to face his men. "Order *Arms!*" he barked.

In perfect unison, a thousand hands dropped salute. Feet hammered and thighs slapped together.

Lt. Col. Alan Caldwell spun about-face to the reviewing stand and thundered, "Sir! First Battalion ready for pass in review!"

The post commander returned the salute. "Colonel. Pass in review."

Spinning again, eyes flashing in the brisk salted air, Caldwell bellowed: "Company commanders. Pass in review!"

On that cue, the band broke into a stirring rendition of "Honor Thy Nation". Under the direction of shouting company commanders, the battalion filed past the reviewing stand in Close Order Drill. Drums cracked, cymbals clashed, and men turned into perfectly geared machines in a dazzling spectacle of pageantry and color honoring hundreds of years of glory and tradition. Bright-eyed and stalwart they passed, row on endless row—America's finest.

The colonel's daughter and an ex-sergeant major stood watching from a hilltop. When the last chord of music had drifted off toward the Pacific, they walked down the other side of the hill, toward the cemetery. It was a favorite spot for both of them, for Donna since she was a little girl and for the sergeant since he'd come back from Vietnam. It was a place to go to think about important things. Life. The neat rows of identical white gravestones reminded them that life was brief and the most one could hope to leave behind was a statement of courage and sacrifice. It didn't make them feel sad, only serious.

"I love this place," Maclure said. "Soldiers from all the wars trade lies with each other."

They walked in amiable silence. Donna loved her father's old friend; she had always been able to talk to him when she couldn't, for whatever reason, talk to her dad. He told her stories and jokes, and he was wise without ever preaching at her. She didn't say anything, just walked contentedly and listened.

"Soldiers should rest together, you know. They've won their peace. I got a spot picked out for myself right over there." He pointed to a tree that shaded a little corner of the grassy hill.

"I thought the cemetery was closed," she said.

"Oh, yes, they closed it in '62, but I got special permission. I'm going to be right next to a corporal from the Spanish-American War. We're going to trade stories. I'm going to say to him, 'Don't tell me about cannons, boy . . . in 'Nam they had claymors, and AK-47s—those were real weapons.'"

Donna looked out at the view from Maclure's final resting place. "Dad asked you to talk to me, didn't he?" she said.

Maclure shook his head. "No. It was all my idea. He doesn't know diddley." He took Donna's arm, and they moved slowly over the grass to the statue of a soldier, battle flag in hand, watching over fallen comrades. "You two been going the full fifteen rounds every day?" he asked her.

Donna kicked at a leaf that got in her way. "Sometimes it's like talking to a brick wall," she told him.

Maclure nodded. "He sure is one stubborn son of a bitch. But of course, you're not. Right?"

She smiled up at her dear dutch uncle, who had saved her father's life and had felt responsible ever since.

"You like this Austin kid?" Maclure asked her.

"Yes. I do like him."

They reached the edge of the cemetery and turned onto the path leading back through a grove of trees where the stones had lain undisturbed and well tended for more than a hundred years.

"You're sure you're not just seeing this guy

because it pisses your old man off?" Maclure asked gingerly.

Donna shook her head. "That may have been a part of it in the beginning," she confessed. "He wants me to marry Captain Gordon."

"Is that what you want?"

Donna's blood heated up just thinking about it. "Of course not!"

Maclure laughed. "Then let him marry Captain Gordon."

"That's kind of what I told him," she said, grinning. They walked in silence between the graves, with the sunlight darting and dancing through the leaves above them. "This guy is different, Mac. He really is. Tell you the truth, he kind of scares me."

"Why?"

She shrugged. "I don't know. He's just—getting too close, I guess."

Maclure stopped walking. He reached for Donna's hands and looked into her troubled eyes. "You ain't afraid of him," he pronounced quietly. "Let me tell you something. You're afraid of yourself."

She smiled and tried to pull away, but Maclure held onto her hands until she had to look at him again. "I'm ugly, not stupid," he said.

"I think you're gorgeous," Donna burst out. She reached up and kissed his tanned-leather cheek. He patted her shoulder, and they turned and walked some more. After a while, Donna asked, out of the blue, "Am I very much like my mother, Top?"

Maclure thought about it. "Well, she was her. You're you."

"Dad won't talk about her. Every time I mention her, a door just closes."

"He really loved her," Maclure said sadly. "When it happened, something broke. He still hurts, Donna. Maybe all the time."

"He never says anything about it," she told him. It hurt her, too, surely he could see that. Couldn't Top see it even if her dad couldn't?

His answer was slow in coming, and thoughtful. "You know, some people can come right out and say what they feel. It's easy for them. Others can't. They just don't know how."

Donna nodded. "That's my father."

"I'll tell you something else about him. He's the finest man I ever met," Maclure said.

"Yeah. I know."

"Do you?"

She didn't answer.

Maclure stopped walking, put his hands in the pocket of his rust-colored polyester slacks, and took a deep breath. He looked around slowly, at all the rows of headstones. "Donna—do you really understand this place? This burying ground, I mean?"

She followed his glance. Her eyes came back to his, asking what he meant, why he'd changed the subject.

They were standing pretty much square in the center of the cemetery. Maclure took a long look around him. Then he said, "Because that's what he's all about, kiddo. And that's what I'm all about, too." She didn't say anything, knowing he would explain in his own good time.

"You gotta listen to it," he said. "Sometimes I see kids walking through this place, with those midget radios hooked onto their belts, and headphones in their ears. They can't hear anything that's going on here. Besides the fact that they're standing in front of some guy who died in World War II . . . and they're listening to a Japanese radio . . ." He trailed off, lost in irony for a minute.

"You've got to listen when you're here, Donna honey. This is the real stuff here. Try it one day.

You could learn something about your father." Donna looked at him curiously, not really understanding, but she nodded.

"Okay. I will, Top."

"When I check out," Maclure said, "you come visit me. I'll be right over there, next to the corporal."

"All right, Top. Sure I will."

"And promise me you won't be wearing some freaking radio."

"I promise."

"Good."

He took her arm and started down the hill again to the path leading her home.

When they passed the Officers' Club, she saw an MP vehicle parked out front, maybe her dad's. It reminded her that he and Austin were working together—maybe they'd come up with some mutual respect somewhere along the line. Maybe they'd even get to liking each other. Maybe her father would end up wanting her to marry Jay Austin instead of Captain Harold Gordon. Donna had to laugh at herself—such fantasies!

Inside the Officers' Club, stale air and the gloomy echoes of Caldwell's heels along the hallway contrasted jaggedly with the memory of two days before, when cops and CID and lab experts and the coroner and the coroner's assistants and reporters and God knew who had been crowded in there jabbering and making notes and taking flash photos. Now there was only silence in the dingy hallway. He tried the door to the storeroom, which had a printed S.F.P.D. sign nailed to it:

CRIME SCENE
NO UNAUTHORIZED PERSONS ALLOWED

The manager's office door was ajar and brightly lit. Even though it was a clear sunny morning, it didn't show here. The rear quarters of the club were dank and grungy, day or night. Caldwell knocked on the open door and went in. Mueller looked up from his cluttered desk.

"Afternoon, Colonel," he said.

"Don't spill your coffee, Mueller," Caldwell said. A styro cup was precariously balanced on a stack of papers. Old rings from previous coffee breaks decorated the gray metal desk where it was visible. "Do you have the key to the storeroom?" he asked.

"Yes, sir," Mueller told him. He yanked open the sticky top drawer of the desk and rooted around in some nests of paper clips, rubber bands, and ballpoint pens. He came up with a key; Caldwell leaned in and took it from him.

The storeroom was gloomy and ominous—the deserted scene of a two-day-old murder. Stacked cartons and crates and boxes lined the walls. A chalked outline on the grimy floor showed where Patti Jean had been found. There were stacks of supplies for the various functions of the club. There were the two potted palms that had seen better days. Caldwell pocketed the key, shut the door, and moved into the room. He knelt beside the palms, touched the soil in first one, then the other. One was bone dry; the other still moist.

He stood up, leaned against the grimy wall and looked around. Where was the source of water and why only one tree? There was no water cooler in the room, no sink. Just cartons and crates and the two trees and that terrible chalk outline on the floor. He eyed the stacks of boxes, and then started opening a few at random. Cases of beer, different brands. Cartons of peanuts and pretzels. A box of swizzle sticks, a box of cocktail napkins stamped with the

Presidio seal and the words *Officers' Club* written below. Over by the window, stacked cases of Black Mountain Drinking Water. Caldwell opened the top case. All the bottles were sealed. He glanced at the other cases stacked together. "Drawn from bubbling mountain springs," the logo proclaimed. He looked closely at every carton. The moisture in that palm tree had to come from somewhere, and these boxes were the only obvious sources of water. Caldwell checked each one. The glued flaps had been pried open on one of the cartons. He looked inside. It was empty. No sealed bottles, no opened bottles, nothing. Empty. He looked over at the palm tree and wondered whether it lived on a diet of bubbling mountain stream water while its buddy over there gasped for just a drop. Somebody wanting to jettison some water and anywhere would do? But why?

Not much of a clue to anything, maybe not a clue at all. But curious. Damned curious. Well, this was one he didn't have to share with the civilian; it was his turf and he'd play his hunch close to the chest for a while.

CHAPTER 11

T HEO? IT'S AUSTIN again. Any news on the Tokarev slugs? No shit! No *shit!* I knew it! Hot damn, I knew that bastard was involved. Thanks, Theo. You're the greatest ballistics expert since . . . fill in the blank. Got to run, thanks again."

Another phone call, involving a little strategic maneuvering with some old army buddies who were still doing MP out at the Presidio, and Austin had Lawrence in his sights. He just had to wait for the moment and he could nail the bastard. It was Lawrence who had killed Patti Jean, after all.

He couldn't stay still. He hopped in the Dodge and cruised toward Seal Beach. He didn't want to get far from the beeper, but watching the seals cavorting out there on the rocks, listening to their cheery yipping, was always a terrific up. He could use one about now.

He knew enough about human and even military psychology to realize that cutting the colonel out of the action, solving the crime without his help, wouldn't do much for his lovelife with Donna. But on the other hand, revenge was irresistible. And he could imagine a scenario in which the crusty colonel actually respected him and, in fact, congratulated him in public and in front of Donna for having been so plucky, so smart, so—

The beeper went off, shrill and insistent. Cut the daydream, Austin. He pulled over to a phone booth and dashed in, dialed the MP station. "This better be what I think it is," he prayed out loud, slamming the door behind him.

"Hey, Jay, it's Zeke. Take it easy."

"Yeah, okay. Sorry. I'm just real anxious."

"Yeah, and I can guess why. Listen, you know that package you wanted me to locate?"

"Yes."

"Well, you can pick it up in Chinatown, at 1412 Washington. But you'd better hurry. I don't think it's gonna be there long."

Austin grinned. "Thanks, pal. I owe you," he said. He hung up and jumped back into the Dodge. He hit the siren and let it blare until he was far down Kearney, crossing Sacramento heading for Washington. He slowed to a legal limit the last two blocks and cruised to a stop in front of 1412. It was a bar. He was just in time to see Paul Lawrence, in civilian clothes, coming out of the joint. Austin stepped out of his car.

Lawrence strolled over to a big white Buick. He started checking his pockets for the keys, but he never found them. Austin stepped up behind him and grabbed a handful of leather jacket. He spun the pipsqueak colonel around so that he was right in his face. He rammed the bastard up against the Buick.

"Surprise," said Austin. He was gratified to note that Lawrence was scared out of his socks. Terrified. Good.

"You can't arrest me," Lawrence snarled, toughing it out.

"Wrong!" Austin told him. "We're not in the

Presidio, we're out here all alone in the real world. You're on my turf, pal. You're not a colonel out here, you're just another asshole. And I *own* you."

Lawrence stammered when he got hot. "You c-c-can't d-d-do th-th-th—"

Austin didn't hang around waiting for him to finish. He spun the jerk around and slammed his chest against the car. "Guess what? I gotta warrant," he gloated. "I got a slug from your Tokarev. I got a ballistics match that says it was from the gun that killed Patti Jean."

He leaned in so that his face was up close to Lawrence's ear. He whispered savagely, "There's only one thing I want you to do. Resist arrest. I really want you to do it. Just a little. Please?" He kicked the colonel's legs apart. The inside of the skinny shins would be black and blue for a week.

"You have the right to remain silent," Austin said. He reached into his pocket for the cuffs. "You have the right to an attorney. If you can't afford—"

Lunging suddenly to his right, Lawrence caught Austin off guard. Austin reeled backward and lost his balance for a minute. He dropped to one knee. Blood trickled from his nose where the punch had connected. He wiped it with the back of his hand and scrambled to his feet. Lawrence had taken advantage of the momentary diversion to make a run for it. He took off blindly into the street, running like a goddamned chicken in a barnyard, fast and awkward but in no particular direction. Austin heard the screech of brakes like an electric saw and the simultaneous yowl of a car's horn. Lawrence dodged between two cars, both moving. Austin took off after him.

He got to the corner of Grant and Washington and hit the sidewalk, knocking over a couple of tourists. Brilliant yellow and red signs with Chinese characters on them hung from the storefronts and restaurants; the atmosphere of gaiety and exotic treats contrasted sharply with the surge of fright that rippled through their midst. The wiry colonel in leather jacket and chino pants, graying and no longer young, badgered and battered his way through the crowds, shoving aside the pushcarts and racks of novelties. Sensing Austin on his tail, Lawrence dived into a narrow alleyway. It was littered with newspapers and rows and rows of garbage cans from all the restaurants on the block.

There was no way Austin was going to let the weasel out of his clutches. This was the bastard that had insulted Patti Jean and gotten away with it. This was the son of a bitch whose gun killed her. This was the shit-eater who used the Army to shield himself from any goddamned thing he wanted to pull . . . Austin was like an uncaged animal in pursuit of his enemy. He ran hard and silently, gaining on the terrified Lawrence, whose gasps could be heard now as he came close to panic and his lungs desperately fought for more air. He ran into the back door of a restaurant, with Austin close behind.

Past the tiny kitchen, through the narrow hall, crashing over a tray of teacups, Lawrence ran frantically and Austin came up tight behind him. The startled cook and proprietor had no time to react. The door was closed. Lawrence wasted a precious few seconds trying to push it open, but it opened inward, and in desperation he threw himself against the plate glass window. Before the shards had shattered to the ground, Austin was through the window too. The chase went on, down Grant Street, with a leap onto the hood of a hapless little car—crrrrunch, first Lawrence then Austin right behind him—and into Ross Alley.

Not so much an alley as the new world's narrowest commercial street, Ross Alley provides a world-class obstacle course for runners. Trinkets and lanterns and tourists and prostitutes and rare antique dealers are set here, there, and every which way along a path just about wide enough for a rickshaw, although cars do manage to compound the chaos now and then. Lawrence ducked and feinted and swerved and sprinted like a linebacker through the Alley; the complexity of barriers in the path had Austin doing the same buck-and-wing. He was about twenty-five feet behind Lawrence when they emerged from the alley. Lawrence turned the corner and ducked into a narrow one-way street.

A car was barreling through. There was no screech of brakes. There was no blare of a horn. The car was simply a yellow flash. The thud of chrome against bone was horrible. Lawrence catapulted up in the air, crashed onto the roof of the car, and bounced cruelly against the trunk as the car sped forward without slowing. He was dead by the time his head hit the pavement with the awful sound of a melon being dropped from a third-story window.

The car never slowed down. It veered to the right to avoid a line of traffic that had stopped in the narrow street ahead, drivers and passengers turning back to rubberneck in horror. The killer careened up onto the sidewalk. Pedestrians screamed and dove out of the way. The hit-and-run driver made a right turn at the end of the street, back onto the pavement—this time brakes did accompany the human shrieks as a car heading west barely missed getting sideswiped. And then it was gone. All over in a matter of seconds.

Austin had taken a dive into the gutter when he first saw Lawrence hit; he watched all the action from the vantage point of rubbing noses with decayed Chinese cabbages, cigarette butts, used tea leaves, and worse. He rose to his feet and, not stopping to brush himself off, ran over to the colonel's inert body.

Austin was out of breath. He stood there panting and trying to shake the shock out of his brain, figure out what he'd just seen. It had happened so fast that other people on the street were standing in bewilderment, too. As he bent down to check Lawrence for a pulse, the onlookers began to close in. In the distance, he heard a siren approaching.

There was no pulse. Lawrence had found a way to escape the law.

"Shit," Austin said.

People started crowding in now. Austin showed his badge and started taking names and numbers of witnesses. In a minute or two, a black-and-white showed up, its lightbar flashing. It was followed by an ambulance and then two more police cars. They got the traffic moving, cut access to the area, moved the crowd behind barricades—did all the right things. Austin looked at his watch. He waited.

In exactly twelve minutes, an MP vehicle pulled into the street and Caldwell got out.

"You're just in time to say bye-bye to your pal," Austin told him. The ambulance attendants, having pronounced the victim dead on the scene, had straightened out Lawrence's disjointed body so that it would fit onto a stretcher and covered him with a nice white sheet. They were just lifting him when Caldwell strode over, pulled down a corner of the sheet, and took a look at what had once been a face. He threw the sheet back and stomped back toward Austin with a truly fierce look in his eyes. His jaw was steel.

Austin was perched on the trunk of a car that happened to be parked there. He was feeling queasy, whether from the run or the shock or the disappointment, he wasn't sure. But he figured he knew what Caldwell was going to say, and he wished he didn't have to hear it.

"You were supposed to go through me," Caldwell said. Each word was spat out like a bullet. "You gave me your word."

Austin stared straight down between his legs at the gutter, for want of anything better to look at. He brushed a hunk of wilted bok choy from his trouser leg. "He ran. I chased him. What the hell was I supposed to do?"

"You gave me your word." Caldwell's accent had become harsh and clipped. The Brits put a heavy price on stuff like that. Well, what the hell, he was right, in a way. Austin believed that a man's word should be trusted, too. But this time . . . this was different, damn it.

"I got a ballistics match, and a clean bust. He did it. I knew it . . . you didn't want to know it. He did it."

Caldwell put his hands on the roof of the car and leaned on it, not looking at Austin. "Do you realize what you've done?" he asked bitterly.

"Yeah," Austin said. "I caught the guy who shot your MP."

"Can you prove that he pulled the trigger?" Caldwell asked.

"He proved it by running."

Caldwell shook his head, despairing. "All right, can you tell me why he broke into the Officers' Club? Can you?"

Austin didn't say anything. He didn't have an answer to that one, but he was sure as hell they could have got it out of Lawrence. Maybe Caldwell was thinking the same thing. "You can't tell me," he said, "and Lawrence sure as shit can't. You made a clean bust, all right. You're a real prize."

"Lawrence was part of this," Austin insisted. "You were wrong about him."

"I was never wrong about him," Caldwell said firmly. "The truth is, I never liked him."

Austin turned and stared at him. "Then why didn't you back me that time—when I busted him?"

"Because you broke the law," Caldwell explained, as if to a slow learner. "You were the cop, and he was the goddamned bad guy. You still don't get it, do you?"

Behind them, the police were moving the crowd to escort the ambulance out with the body. Austin and Caldwell watched the coroner's deputy get into his car to follow.

"Tell me," Caldwell said quietly, "do you think that Lawrence was the only one involved in all this?"

Austin looked at him. Jesus. He had been so intent on revenge . . . suddenly he felt like a real asshole. He didn't say anything, but apparently Caldwell saw some light in his eyes signifying the brain turning back on, because he kept on talking, sharing information now instead of hashing over mistakes.

"I tried to tell you after we left Peale's office," Caldwell said. "About the coasters on his bar." He waited for the coin to drop.

"Coasters?"

Caldwell nodded. "From the Caravelle Bar in Saigon."

Austin perked up. "Saigon . . ." He was trying to put it together, but the pieces weren't exactly a neat fit, not yet.

"You ran a make on Peale, right?" Caldwell asked.

"Yes. He was clean."

Caldwell shook his head. "You run a make . . .

and you find that the guy has never been convicted of rape, so he's clean. Jesus. Did you check his service record?"

Austin nodded. "He wasn't in the service."

"He wasn't in the service," Caldwell repeated thoughtfully, "and he's got souvenirs from Vietnam."

Austin shrugged. "So the guy collects coasters."

Caldwell took a cigar out of his pocket. The crowd was starting to disperse, and the black-and-whites were down to two. The street was still blocked off, but there was not much to see. Another chalk outline marking another dead body; two photographers, one from the city and one from a newspaper, a couple of reporters asking questions. Austin recognized the owner of the restaurant excitedly explaining to Detective Manning—with gestures—how his plate glass had been broken. Judging by Manning's sympathetic nods and voluminous note taking, it looked like Austin would probably have to show up at a hearing before the city would pick up the tab for that.

Caldwell finally got the stogie lit and puffing. "I ran a check of my own on Peale," he told Austin. "Through my own sources. The guy was CIA. He was a province adviser in Long Binh at the same time Lawrence was stationed there."

"They knew each other?" Austin asked.

"What the hell do you think?" Caldwell said. He chewed down hard on his cigar.

Austin started thinking out loud, excited now. "Whoever broke into the Officers' Club storeroom was looking for something. Something they wanted real bad . . ."

Caldwell raised one eyebrow, encouraging his slow pupil to keep on thinking. He puffed and chomped and listened as Austin started making connections.

"Christ . . . the water!" Austin yelped. "There were two plants in the storeroom but only one had water in it. The other one was dry."

"Correct," said Caldwell. "And one of the water cases in that storeroom was empty, only it wasn't Mueller who opened it."

"What about Mueller?" Austin asked him.

"No, he's got an alibi. I checked it myself. Anyway, why would he break in? He has a key." Caldwell turned and started walking, and Austin scrambled off the car to keep up with him. They sauntered closer to the scene of the accident and stood staring down at the bloody spot where Lawrence had bought it.

"What the hell could have been in that bottle—besides the water that got dumped in the tree?" Austin mused.

"If you're interested," Caldwell said, inhaling his foul cigar, "I have the address of the water company. They open at 0900."

"I'll pick you up at eight-thirty," Austin said. "Your quarters."

Caldwell grunted and nodded and chomped down on his cigar and walked away. Austin watched a photographer take one last angle, pack up his camera, and get into his car. Everything was already back to normal. Cars were rolling over the chalkmark now. Caldwell's MP vehicle backed over it and moved into the stream of traffic.

Austin realized he wanted to apologize for being such a hardhead, and stupid on top of that. "Hey . . ." he started to call to Caldwell, but it was too late.

CHAPTER 12

SANTA CLARA IS San Francisco's version of Magic Mountain or any of the thousands of amusement parks around the country: no special theme, just rides and games of chance and skill and the kind of good old-fashioned cons that Americans love. For a lot of dollars you can have a few laughs and go home with a plaster pig or a stuffed moose that's uglier than your Uncle Jake. You can cram yourself with scorched, half-raw hot dogs, cotton candy guaranteed to make your teeth rot, too much lousy beer. You stand in line for the privilege of riding on gravity-defying rides rigged with scotch tape and bobby pins, just so you can find out which comes first: throwing up, getting killed, or your having your three-minutes-for-a-buck-and-a-half run out. It's fun, it's silly, it's scary, it's traditional. That's where a cop takes a girl for a date when he's kind of nuts about her. Jay Austin was there, wearing a paper derby hat five sizes too small, carrying an outsized teddy bear, and holding the hand of a girl he was getting kind of nuts about.

The only thing was, he wasn't laughing. Not even

smiling. He couldn't stop thinking about what an asshole he'd been that day. Losing Lawrence like that—for good, and before he talked . . . and letting his single-minded pursuit of that miserable son of a bitch cloud his mind so that he really appeared like a dumb jerk-off to Caldwell, whom he suddenly found himself admiring, kind of. And here he was with Caldwell's daughter, when suddenly the absolute last thing he wanted was to totally lose the old man's respect . . .

"Come on, Austin. Lighten up," Donna prodded. She put her arm through his. Her tangled yellow hair flew behind her in a carefree gust of wind and she laughed at the way he looked in his fine new hat. Austin smiled at her abstractedly, not light at all.

Suddenly she stopped and looked up. "Let's go on that thing," she said, pulling at his arm. Austin looked up and up and up at the Ferris wheel. It was very high from down on the ground, which is where any sensible person would stay. Looking up at the swinging cars was as close as he ever cared to get to that diabolic instrument of torture.

"That?" he asked.

She nodded excitedly and tugged at his arm. "C'mon."

"Uh-uh," he told her, shaking his head. "I don't think so. No. No, you go ahead. I'll watch. I'll wait for you right here, I won't budge an inch."

"Oh, come on!" she urged him.

"That's okay, you go," he said. "Here, I'll buy you a ticket and—"

"No, no, come on with me!" she pleaded.

"I don't want to."

"Why not?"

"I—don't like heights. That's all. No big deal."

"You're afraid." She just stated it, not accusing, not laughing at him, just rather incredulous.

"I'm not afraid," he explained patiently. "I just don't like being up high. It makes me dizzy, that's all. Something to do with the inner ear, you know, something like that. It's not abnormal. Lots of people—"

"You're afraid," she said again.

"No, believe me, that's not it at all . . ."

She pulled him over to the ticket booth and he bought two tickets and the first thing he knew he was sitting in the chair with her. It was very tippy. The man belted them in, but the thing was very rickety, really.

"I really don't want to do this," he said, almost pleading.

"You've got to confront your fear," Donna told him.

"Who says?"

She nodded wisely. "Everybody," she said. "Doctors. It's in all the psychology books. Look it up. If you have a fear, you must confront it."

Suddenly, she unbelted herself and jumped out of the gondola. He was relieved and reached for his buckle, but she pushed him back into the seat. "Wait here, I'll be right back!" she shouted. She stepped down to the man who was about to operate the switch. She said something to him. The operator looked over at Austin and then grinned and nodded to Donna. Austin desperately wanted to escape. But Donna was back in a second, climbing in next to him and fastening up.

"Thanks!" she shouted to the operator as he threw the switch and started them on the death-defying upward swing. The gondola swayed in the wind. Austin was shaking like a leaf.

"C-can we talk about this?" he pleaded. His hands hurt already from holding onto the bar so tightly, and they had only begun to climb. Donna giggled. "Oh, shit," Austin said, looking down at the disappearing ground. The gondola was swinging in a way that seemed downright irresponsible.

Instead of talking, Donna was getting goofy. She leaned to him, and kissed his neck, and then his ear, all the while her hand was unbuttoning his shirt. "Just relax," she told him huskily. "Whatever you do, don't look down."

He looked down. Vertigo hit him like a sledgehammer. The ground fell away and nothing was in its place; the horizon swayed and bobbed and weaved. There was nothing to focus on. The gondola was swinging madly back and forth, tipping them ass over elbow, and all the while Donna was making him wild with what she was doing to his ear. He was swooning. He was being blitzed by conflicting sensations, dizzy and scared and drowning in her caresses. She had his shirt completely unbuttoned and they were still ascending on a wide arc, still swinging back and forth. His emotions and physical responses swung back and forth too, and he was totally helpless not knowing if he was going to die or go to heaven.

"No!" he protested weakly. His hands grabbed the sides of the flimsy car with a death grip. But the rest of his body seemed to be responding to the sexual excitement.

"Don't look down," she breathed moistly into his ear.

"Oh, God! Woooooo . . . !"

"Uh, huh," she murmured into his neck. She began unbuckling his belt. The gondola kept climbing higher and higher until it was suspended in space with no apparent means of support, swaying wickedly. She bit his nipple. He didn't know any longer where he was, only that he was off the planet earth. He didn't know what was going to happen, except that it was going to be the last experience of his life.

When they reached the top of the Ferris wheel, out of sight of anyone else in the world, the operator stopped the motion and let them hang there, swaying silently. Or it should have been silently—in fact, moaning and sighing and kissing sounds wafted out of the gondola into the evening air.

Austin was a wreck. He couldn't move and couldn't control the sexual excitement of his body, but terror kept him from being able to let go of his grip on the gondola. Frantic to get at him, Donna unlatched and pushed aside the safety bar. She clambered on top of him.

From a hundred feet below, anyone who cared to look up might wonder why the topmost gondola on the Ferris wheel was rocking more wildly than the others, propelled by some force other than the wind. Austin's silly little paper derby hat sailed earthward, tumbling like a leaf, tossed on the wind until it disappeared into the throng of people on the midway.

When his feet landed on firm ground again, Austin didn't know whether to be glad or sorry.

"See what happens when you face your fears?" Donna teased him as they walked away, arms around each other. He was glad of her arm around his waist—he needed the support.

"I'm glad I waited," he told her. Laughing like kids without a care, they headed for the tunnel of love.

Austin was relieved to realize that he didn't feel guilty at all when he picked up Caldwell the next morning. What he and Donna had going was in a class by itself; he had never experienced such pleasure in another person's company—yes, it was sexual, but it was a whole lot more than that, in ways he wasn't ready to explore just yet. But he knew that continuing to see her was high priority in his life and it was just too damned bad if the colonel got pissed off about it. It was between him and Donna. He did wish there was some way to clear the air between Caldwell and himself, though —on a professional level, if not a personal one.

They drove into the industrial district, where the flat streets formed a grid between warehouses, garages, factories, offices, and an occasional flophouse or mission. The Black Mountain Water Company couldn't be missed—a huge sign along the whole side of a block-long building. Austin parked in the guest parking lot and they headed for the main entrance.

"Follow my lead, okay?" Austin said, hoping to sound friendly but firm.

Caldwell, all decked out in his nicely pressed uniform with the braid on his cap and the medals on his chest, wasn't having any. "No," he said, "it's not okay. I'd like to know how you're going to handle it."

"Look, we don't want to tip anybody off," Austin explained. "I happen to be good at this, okay?"

Caldwell didn't acknowledge that. He walked into the building, with Austin a step ahead. A foyer opened into several rooms, each with a little sign jutting out over its door. They bypassed RECEPTION and went into DISPATCH ROOM. It was a small, well lit, square room. An attempt had been made, with more passion than taste, to decorate the place. A potted ficus tree in need of light, a glass-topped desk and a couple of chairs, walls almost completely covered with livid posters of rock stars. The young woman behind the desk was in her twenties, rail thin, with a slightly zoned-out expression on her face. Little headphones were stuck in her ears, attached to a Walkman on the desk. She was rubber-stamping a stack of papers in time to a rhythm only she could hear.

Austin motioned Caldwell to wait, let him handle this. Caldwell didn't like the idea any more now than he had a minute before. He frowned. Austin stopped in his tracks and so did Caldwell. They stared each other down. The receptionist didn't appear to notice them at all. Let me handle it, Austin pleaded with his eyes. Caldwell's chin toughened up a notch, his eyes glinted, and he stood his ground. Then he relented, with a softening around his mouth and eyes. Austin nodded, a sort of thanks, but not quite. He walked over to the desk. DISPATCHER was written on a little fake-bronze plaque on her desk.

He stood at the edge of the desk until she looked up. Her first look was blank; she was still tuned in to her solitary concert. Then she registered Austin, frankly appraising him from head to crotch. She liked what she saw and didn't mind letting on.

"Awwwright!" she said softly.

Austin smiled, pointed to her headphones. She took them off, a bit sheepishly.

"I'm looking for the dispatcher," he told her.

"You've found her, man. Her name is Gloria," the young woman said, giving him her best smile.

Austin was aware of Caldwell prowling the room behind him, sniffing things out. Austin ignored him and leaned forward onto Gloria's desk, ostensibly to study the posters on the wall behind her. "You follow the Dead?" he asked.

"Everywhere, man," Gloria told him with a sigh. "You too?"

Austin went a bit dreamy. "First time I was with

them was Winterland, '78. I flipped. Been with them ever since," he confided.

"Wow."

"Did you do Oakland last New Year's?" Austin asked her.

Gloria beamed proudly. "All six shows. I slept in the parking lot." She sighed with the pleasure of her memories. "It was soooo mellow," she said.

Caldwell was edging closer, trying to understand what the hell they were talking about. Austin wanted to laugh but managed not to. He sat on the edge of Gloria's desk, pushing aside a pile of papers. She didn't mind in the least. He just hoped the old man was learning a thing or two. "How many shows have you seen?" he asked the wide-eyed Gloria.

"Anaheim was a hundred seventy-nine," she told him. "My boyfriend hasn't missed one for four years. I can't do that, 'cause of work, you know. I mean, I'm here, like, all the time, you know? My boyfriend's old man's got money. Work's such a drag, you know."

"I know," Austin agreed.

"I'd follow the Dead anywhere. They even did Egypt. Did you know that? I woulda followed them to Egypt. Anywhere, man."

Austin nodded. "The Pyramid concert, '78. The best one I've ever been to," he said. He was conscious of Caldwell a few steps behind him, making impatient little snorting and grunting noises. No finesse, the colonel. One thing the Army didn't teach its officers was finesse. Let him watch how a pro did it.

Gloria's little round red mouth was hanging open. "You were *there?*" she gasped.

Austin nodded modestly. "Well . . . Jerry Garcia is kind of a friend," he lied.

Gloria was impressed. "Wow, that is completely out of sight!" she exclaimed. Her eyes shone as she looked up at Austin with something close to worship. Then she leaned over to him, lowered her voice, and pointing to Caldwell with one thumb, she asked, "Who's General Washington?"

Austin lowered his voice too. "He's my father," he told her.

Gloria showed her sympathy with a knowing, understanding nod. "Bummer," she said.

"Tell me about it," Austin agreed.

"He into elevator music?" she asked.

Austin made a face. "What do you think?" He leaned forward, getting very close to her now. "Listen, Gloria," he confided. "This is really kinda embarrassing. Last week I borrowed my father's car. I parked it outside the Officers' Club at the Presidio. When I came out, somebody had banged into it. I mean, no big deal, you know. Right? Well, I thought I saw one of your water trucks making a delivery. I thought maybe the driver had seen something, you know . . . if I could talk to him—" Austin broke off, and motioned toward Caldwell, who was looking more menacing every minute as he paced the room, stopping every few feet to stare back at the two of them. It was pretty obvious he was mad and getting madder. "He doesn't believe me," Austin told Gloria's willing ear. "He thinks I wrecked it."

Gloria tore her eyes away from Austin's to sneak another look at Caldwell's hawklike profile. "He never believes you, right?" she said.

Austin shrugged. "Is yours any different?"

Gloria understood perfectly. She sighed and turned to a Rolodex. She flipped it and started digging through the cards. "Listen, you didn't get this from me, okay?" Austin nodded, showing his

126

gratitude with his eyes. Gloria got the message. She found the card she was looking for. "Officers' Club at the Presidio . . . deliveries are Tuesdays and Saturdays. Driver's name is Spota."

"Is he working today?" Austin wanted to know.

Gloria shook her head. "It's his day off. You can catch him at eight-thirty in the morning."

Austin nodded. "Does he have a first name?" he asked.

"Do you?" Gloria countered.

He grinned. "Jay."

She nodded, smiling. "Spota's first name is George. I like yours better."

He leaned in so close he was practically whispering into her ear. "Listen . . . I know this is asking a lot . . . but . . . well, hey, do you think you could give me his address? I promise no hassles."

Gloria hesitated. "I don't know, man," she said reluctantly.

Austin flipped his thumb in Caldwell's direction again. "Take a good look at him," he told her. "Does he look like someone who will wait till tomorrow morning?"

Gloria looked over at Caldwell. He was standing in front of an old Stones poster, glaring at it ferociously. She looked back at Austin. She dropped a huge sigh and went back to the Rolodex card. "732 Vermont," she whispered. "You never heard it from me, right?"

Austin slowly got to his feet. "Thanks, Gloria," he said. "Hey, if I sent you something here, would it get to you at this address? A friend of mine made a bootleg tape of the Garden concert. I'll send it to you."

Gloria was thrilled. Her mouth opened like a bubble-gum balloon. "Oh, wow, I don't know what to say, man!" she crooned.

Austin backed off, grinning. "That's okay. Us Deadheads have to stick together."

He turned and started to walk over to Caldwell, who was at the door.

"Later," Gloria sang out after him.

Austin nodded and waved. Just as he reached Caldwell, Gloria called out, "Hey, General!"

Caldwell turned. "Colonel," he said drily.

Gloria smiled. "You really ought to lighten up," she advised him, as friendly as could be.

Lt. Col. Alan Caldwell thought this over for a second, then nodded briskly. "I'll try," he agreed.

Austin tried not to laugh as they walked back to the car. "The guy who delivers water to the Officers' Club is named Spota," he told Caldwell.

"George Spota?"

He was full of surprises. "How'd you know?" Austin asked.

"He was a master sergeant. He served at Long Binh. Under Lawrence," Caldwell said.

Austin whistled low, under his breath. "Today's his day off," he told Caldwell. "He starts work at eight-thirty tomorrow morning. By the way, water was delivered to the Presidio the same day Patti Jean was killed."

They got into the Dodge. Austin started it up, pulled out of the lot, and headed north.

Caldwell seemed preoccupied, so Austin kept quiet too, thinking things out. They were definitely making connections, but what could it add up to? What was in the water besides water? His thoughts were interrupted when Caldwell spoke up.

"What the hell is the Dead?"

Austin grinned. "Oh, well, I don't think you'd understand if I told you," he said.

"Try me," Caldwell snapped.

"The Grateful Dead," Austin explained.

"The Grateful Dead," Caldwell repeated, no more enlightened than he had been a second before.

"The Grateful Dead," Austin echoed, as if that settled it.

A minute passed before Caldwell said, "I don't understand."

"I didn't think you would," Austin pointed out. Then he took pity on the guy, leaned over and opened the glove compartment, rooted around until he found a Dead cassette, and handed it to the colonel. Caldwell looked at the label, read it thoroughly, and then put it back in the glove compartment, slamming the door shut.

"There's something I want to check out when I get back," Caldwell said, as if thinking out loud.

"What is it?" Austin asked.

"I'll tell you tomorrow."

Austin did a fast burn. That was a lousy way to treat a guy who had just done some pretty clever uncovering and shared it all . . . well, if the colonel wanted to play, what the hell. "Good," Austin said. "There's something *I* want to check out."

Caldwell started to ask, but stopped himself.

"Tomorrow," Austin said. Maybe it was his imagination, but he thought he heard Caldwell's teeth gnashing, just a little.

CHAPTER 13

CALDWELL PICKED UP the phone in his study and dialed Langley, Virginia. When the operator answered with the number only, he asked to be connected to Public Relations. Another noncommittal operator, this time a man. He asked for Gareth Wootton.

After a moment's wait, he heard his old friend's voice come on. "Wootton here."

"Alan Caldwell," he said genially. "How are you, Gar?"

"Hey, great to hear from you. I'm fine, how about you, old buddy?"

"Fine. How are things out there?"

"Couldn't be better. Great to hear your voice. You enjoying the California sunshine and all those gorgeous surfers out there? What a post!"

"Oh, yeah, it's terrific," Caldwell assured him heartily. He looked out of the window; a couple of golfers were chopping their way out of a sand trap. "Hey, you'd better be careful, Gar, you'll get sores on your ass from sitting behind a desk too long."

"Well, you watch mine and I'll watch yours," his friend chuckled.

"Listen, I need a favor." Caldwell got to the point, since the Army was paying for the call. "There's a holding company out here called Transcorp," he said. "T-R-A-N—"

"I can spell. Transcorp. With an "s" on the end or not?"

"Not. More like corporation than Army corps."

"Got it. So?"

"So push one of those buttons and tell me what companies they own," Caldwell said.

"Hold on. I got this computer can do it while you wait."

"Right."

Caldwell didn't have to wait more than a few seconds; his friend at the CIA came back with detailed information, which he scribbled down as fast as it came over the wire. "Thanks," he said, "I really appreciate it. Give my love to Linda."

"Okay, now we're even, right?"

Caldwell laughed. "No, hell, we're not even. Tell her she made a mistake. I am much better looking."

He hung up the phone. Donna was standing at the door to his study, looking very pretty in a black dress that he wished had a higher neckline. "Hi, sweetheart, where you going looking so pretty?"

Donna laughed. "To the beach."

"Like that?"

"Well, I was supposed to have a lunch date at the Top of the Mark, but it got canceled so . . . I'm just going for a walk."

"Somebody stood you up?" Caldwell was ready to be enraged.

"No. He'll meet me as soon as he can get away. Don't worry so much, Dad."

"You mean don't pry into your business so much?"

Donna smiled and came into the room. She leaned over his desk and kissed him. "Something like that," she agreed. "'Bye. See you later."

She drove to Baker's Beach and parked along the ridge leading down through pine trees to the dunes. She sat for a long time pleasantly musing in the sun, then she got up to take a walk. She strolled at the edge of the water, carrying her shoes in one hand. She loved the feeling of the waves washing gently over her tanned bare feet. She and Jay Austin had had a date for lunch, but then he'd gotten caught up in his work and said he'd call her when he was free. Instead, she asked him to meet her at the beach. She'd driven straight over and had spent most of that afternoon pleasantly quiet, thinking about him, enjoying the glorious view, listening to the birds and the gentle Pacific waves. Baker's Beach was just about her favorite place in the world. Anyway, she didn't want to be anywhere near a phone, waiting for it to ring. She padded barefoot in the wake of the outgoing tide, making footprints that were instantly wiped away as each new wave tossed up treasures from the sea: shells, white stones and tiny glinting pebbles, pieces of driftwood, bits of colored glass that had been dropped from a ship or a boat years before and tossed in the salty waves for so long they were smooth and opaque. Off to the left, she could see the Golden Gate Bridge, with the foamy afternoon fog just starting to gather behind it. Old pines and cypress trees sheltered the dunes; beyond them lay the Spring Valley Pumping Station that had once served all of San Francisco. Now it supplied only the Presidio. From Fort Point to Seacliff, this stretch of beach was public, but no matter how many other people came here it was never crowded.

Most of the sunbathers, strollers, rockhounds, shell collectors, bass fishermen, shouting children, and gamboling dogs had packed up and left by the time Austin showed up. He ran across the sand to her, and they walked together along the edge. Donna laughed with delight, feeling that her beautiful day was now perfect.

They held hands, stopping now and then to pick up a treasure as it washed up from the deep. The sun was still warm. The city of San Francisco shimmered across the water when the beach curved around. A sign in the dunes above them announced that anyone passing this point was entering the Presidio.

"When I was sixteen, all I wanted was to get away from here," Donna told him. "I just never realized how beautiful it is."

Austin didn't answer. He gripped her hand and stooped for a starfish. It was probably dead, but he tossed it back into the waves. They kept on walking.

"What are you thinking about?" Donna asked.

"How beautiful it is," Austin answered.

"And?"

"And . . . how beautiful you are."

She laughed delightedly. "And?"

"And . . . how beautiful I am."

"And?" she prompted.

"How beautiful we are," they sang out in perfect unison. She had managed to coax a laugh out of him. He was very serious today, in his dark suit and tie and white button-down shirt.

"What else?" she asked.

"Oh . . . stuff."

Donna nodded. "Stuff . . . I see . . . cops-and-robbers stuff?"

"A little," he admitted. He picked up a clamshell and skimmed it across the water.

"And maybe a little you-and-me stuff?" Donna prodded.

"A little of that," he agreed.

"You'll be there tonight, won't you?" she asked.

Austin took a deep breath. Sea air, nothing like it to clear your head. "I may be a little late," he told her. "There's something I have to do."

"But . . . you will be there, won't you?"

Austin made a face. They stopped walking and faced each other. The sun was touching down on the edge of the world, turning the sky rosy and lavender. "I hate that place," Austin said.

"It's just dinner and the usual Friday night dance. What's to hate?" She kicked at a broken clamshell.

"It's the Officers' Club." He said it as if the words could burn his mouth if he didn't spit them out fast.

Donna laughed. "Well, you're not exactly re-enlisting if you go to dinner and have a dance or two there."

"I hate officers," he said, from the heart.

"Please?"

He hesitated. "Couldn't we go someplace else, just the two of us? Anyplace else?" he suggested, but he had a hunch she wouldn't bite.

"Be a sport?" she wheedled.

Austin looked at her. The lowering sun was making her golden hair shine like a halo. How could anybody that angelic looking be such a devil? He couldn't resist kissing her, just once. Well, twice.

"If I show up," he told her, "I'm not going to dance with any officers."

She hugged him tightly. The tide was coming in and the water lapped around their legs. His shoes and socks and trousers were soaked, but what the hell.

"Maybe one dance," he conceded. "Not a slow one, though."

He kissed her again. Suddenly, he felt terrific.

"Let's go for a swim," he suggested, with a bit of the devil in him, too. Maybe it was catching.

Donna shook her head. "The water's too cold," she said.

"It's not that bad. Invigorating," he said.

Donna pulled back. "I don't want to," she said.

"Why not?" He was surprised. In every encounter so far, she had been the leader, the one who goaded him into doing things he didn't think he could or would . . . the ride in the Ferris wheel was one thing he'd never forget. But Donna looked strange . . . nervous? Hey, now, what was this? Austin probed a bit. "Why not?" he repeated.

"I just don't want to," she said.

"Be a sport."

"No."

This was very, very interesting. The wild chick was suddenly a small golden thing with ruffled feathers.

"Why?" Austin persisted.

Donna shrugged. She kicked at a sand dollar. She rolled her toe in the sand. She looked over at the sunset, now streaking the whole sky with color. He just waited.

"I can't swim," she finally admitted, looking down at her toes.

He looked at her thoughtfully. It began to dawn

on her what he was thinking. Frowning, she backed away from him. Austin grinned.

"You're afraid of the water," he said.

"I didn't say that."

Austin took a step toward her, grinning like a kid. "Got to confront your fears," he said.

"Wait—" Squealing, she turned and raced back up the beach. He charged after her. She was fast. He was faster. He lunged forward to tackle her and brought her down onto the soft white sand. She squirmed under him, trying to bite whatever part of him she could make contact with.

"It's in all the psychology books," Austin told her, laughing. "You've got to confront your fears."

"Let me go, damn it!" Donna yelped.

Austin shook his head, holding her down with an easy grip. "No way," he told her. With that, he scooped her up into his arms and got to his feet. He carried her toward the water. Her eyes were wide and she was truly frightened. She hung onto him and screamed. "Wait! Wait, damn it! It's not funny!"

He carried her right into the surf. She pulled his hair. A wave slammed into them, drenching them both, clothes and all. Hanging onto his neck for dear life, Donna gulped at the air. She was terrified.

"It'll be okay," Austin said, mimicking the way she had said the same words the night of the Ferris wheel. "I'll help you."

She clung to him desperately. The surf roiled and thundered. The sky was turning purple. The huge fireball of sun touched down on the horizon and was reflected in the water like an omen of apocalypse. Donna was terrified, and she attacked the only way she knew. She squirmed in his arms until she was facing him, then she slid down his body.

Her voice was hoarse with fear. "You wanna play?" she shouted desperately. "Let's play!"

There was madness in her eyes, blazing despite the salt water. Her hair was drenched and her dress was clinging to every dimple of her body. Curling her lip, she kissed him passionately, grinding her body into him like a steam drill.

He couldn't believe what was happening. But it happened. The Pacific roared and crashed around them. Austin managed to keep them both afloat while the waves thrusted and peaked and pulled them toward the shore, where they would be tossed, spent and fulfilled once more.

Soaked to the skin and trailing seaweed, locked in each other's arms and exhausted, they lay on the sand until the sun was gone. The fog descended, bringing the chill of the night down on them. They stood up, a bit shaky. Austin had lost a shoe, Donna had seaweed tangled in her hair. They brushed each other and laughed and kissed a lot, and then she shivered and they ran up through the evergreens on the embankment. Their cars were the only ones still parked along Gibson's Road. Cutting through the gap in the fence, they didn't stop to read the signs warning the public to beware the undertow and the sharks.

"See you tonight?" she asked.

"Come with me someplace else? Anyplace else?" he asked, one more time.

Donna shook her head. Austin sighed and nodded. "I've got some work to do first, but I'll be there. Later."

She kissed him. It was salty and she looked a mess, and he loved it a lot. She drove off and he squished with his one shoe and dripping blue suit into his Dodge. He smiled all the way home. Once there, he threw the wet clothes in the bathtub and put on some dry stuff as quickly as he could. Ravenous, he grabbed a chicken leg from the take-out barbecue he'd brought home a couple of nights before. Then he went out to the car. He brought along a bath towel to sit on, the driver's seat being a bit on the damp side.

He drove to Vermont Street and slowed down, looking for number 732. It was one of the original old residential streets of San Francisco, with rows of attached houses alternating with once-elegant two-story Victorian houses now turned into apartments. He found a parking space in the 700 block and got out, walking down to 732. It was one of the attached variety, no particular character, built maybe in the fifties, painted white and kept in reasonably good condition. He looked at the mailbox out front: SPOTA. There was a car in the driveway, a blue Trans-Am. He went over to it, tried the door.

It was locked. The car was immaculate. Not a dent on it. He was disappointed. He didn't know what he hoped to find, but finding nothing was always a disappointment. He turned to go back to his car, but then it occurred to him that the Trans Am was a little bit too perfect. On a hunch, he walked back to it. He didn't want to use his flashlight, but there was enough light from the streetlamp. He crouched down so that he couldn't be seen from the house, reached in his pocket and came up with his keys. With surgical delicacy, he scraped at the edge of the fender.

The blue paint came away and revealed yellow underneath.

He was practically whistling as he got into his car and pulled away. He smiled to himself, heading back to his place. He thought about Donna and the violent, wonderful crashing of the surf; he thought about the wild, swinging Ferris wheel. This was some crazy wonderful woman . . . maybe more crazy than wonderful. But then he remembered how fantastic it had been, and it promised to be more of the same, so he figured he'd probably follow her anywhere. Look at him now, actually going home to get dressed so he could go to the Officers' Club!

CHAPTER 14

DONNA WAS PLAYING some kind of nasty game and Austin was fit to split. He sat at the table alone, letting his eyes roam the room rather than stare (as her father was doing, somewhat to the annoyance of the ripe and fully matured luscious redhead at Caldwell's own table) at Donna, dancing a whole lot closer than necessary with an asshole captain. His instincts were always right, and this one had said *Avoid Officers' Clubs* in neon across his forehead, but had he noticed? Not enough to slow down. So here he was twizzling his swizzle stick, surrounded on all sides by Army brass and their wives and friends.

Attempts had been made to turn the Officers' Club into a habitat for humans. The tables had white cloths on them. Here and there, mostly in corners, live palm trees fought bravely against insurmountable odds the losing battle for light and breathable air. The bar was long and made out of bamboo. The dance floor was a good size, and the band was lively and professional. It might have been a perfectly okay place except for three things:

(1) the joint was full of Army brass and their wives; (2) Alan Caldwell was sitting a few tables away with a good-looking redhead but his eyes were on (3) Donna dancing a lot closer than she needed to with one Captain Harold Gordon. Austin sat at a table for two and played with the twizzler in his drink. It said "United States Sixth Army" on it and he was trying to sink it.

The music finally ended and the spit-and-polish creep captain with the self-satisfied smile moved with his arm still around Donna back toward Austin. He stopped and said something in her ear that made her laugh, and then the captain turned back to his buddies. Finally, Donna came toward him on her own. She sat down still smiling, flushed from the terrific fun it all seemed to be.

"Can we leave now?" Austin asked.

"But I just ordered this drink," she said, laughing at nothing. Or at him.

Why was she doing this? Why had she dragged him here to watch how popular she was, how much she didn't give a damn what he was feeling? Why— oh, shit, he couldn't believe he was falling for it. She was just playing cheap old see-how-I-can-make-you-jealous tricks. His chest felt heavy from the weight of his disappointment. He really had thought she was different. Special. That all her sexy tricks were invented for him alone. Smart, Austin. Real smart.

"Can we please leave?" he said again, not smiling.

Before she could frame an answer, the West Point wonder was back at their table, his spit-polished teeth gleaming in the candlelight. "May I have this dance?" he asked, ignoring Austin.

"Give it a rest," Austin told him shortly.

"Captain Gordon, did you know that Inspector

Austin is a policeman?" Donna said in a mock-serious tone. She giggled drunkenly.

The captain offered his hand to Donna. She flashed a cheery look over at Austin and stopped giggling when she saw his eyes flash furiously. She didn't get up right away, but she left her hand in the captain's. Austin had the strong feeling that Caldwell was eyeing this scene with more than passing interest.

"I want to go now, Donna. Please." he said firmly, for the last time.

She put on an impish grin. "You're being impolite," she told him.

The captain decided it was his business. "You don't like it here?" he remarked down his nose at Austin.

"No, I don't, dickhead!" Austin snapped.

Donna laughed. Usually he loved the sound of her laughing, but this time he didn't love it one damn bit.

"What did you say?"

Well, at least he had offended the offensive captain. Gordon dropped Donna's hand and stood there looking like he might slap Austin's face with a glove, if he had a glove. Austin saw Donna sneaking a look over toward the table where Caldwell was sitting with the sexy redhead, and all of a sudden he had to wonder whether this act was for his sake or her father's. In either case, he didn't like it.

"What the hell are you doing?" he asked Donna quietly. "I don't want to play this game."

"I asked you a question, mister," the captain snapped.

"I heard you," Austin said, but he didn't take his eyes off Donna. "You just gotta push it, don't you?" he said sadly. "Everything, right up to the edge."

"Maybe you and I should step outside?" the captain was sneering.

Still looking at Donna, who had averted her eyes, Austin said, "Is this what you want? I'm supposed to fight this jerk for your hand?" She didn't answer or look at him. He sighed and looked up at the double bars. "You want to step outside and settle this like gentlemen?" he asked.

"However you like."

"Marquis of Queensbury rules," Austin suggested. He swung around in his seat as if to get up, but instead his foot kicked out and connected with the captain's privates. It was totally unexpected and a devastatingly low blow. Captain Gordon keeled over forward, groaning and holding his hands over his testicles, although it was clearly too late to help.

"That what you wanted to see?" he asked Donna.

The music stopped with a sour blare from the trumpet. Pandemonium flipped the whole room. People at tables leaped to their feet, craning to see. The dancers stopped and stared. Whispers, a couple of screams, a lot of jabber and, as the wave went through the Sixth Army, several macho officers started moving in close. Austin looked around; Caldwell was advancing on him like he wanted to kill. Bare hands.

"Easy, Colonel," Austin told him. "I'm finished."

He reached into his pocket and came up with his wallet, counted out some bills, and dumped them on the table. At his feet, the captain groaned and rolled onto his side, pulling his knees up in a fetal position. Austin stepped over him and looked back ruefully at Donna. Then he spoke to her father, more or less a formal answer to a formal question.

"Whatever my intentions were, you can forget 'em," he said. "She's too dangerous."

The music started again and everyone in the place began to settle down. The provost marshal was on the job; anyway, it was all over except for the sight of Captain Gordon still rolling on the floor with his pain. Austin started to leave. Donna got to her feet to follow him. Her father grabbed her arm and, although she tried, she couldn't shake him off. He waited until Austin was well away, and then escorted Donna gently but firmly out of there and home.

Neither of them said anything in the car. They were eons apart, thinking their separate thoughts. I've done it all wrong, Caldwell was thinking. I've made a botch of being both parents to her, I don't know what to do now and if her life is a shambles she would be right to blame me, but how the hell do you bring up a girl without a mother? I've never known the right thing to do for her and I guess I never will; bringing up a daughter is a hell of a lot harder than running a goddamned army. And Donna was thinking, why did I act so bitchy, what gets into me sometimes, now I've lost Austin and made my dad mad at me too, and I sure as hell didn't get what I wanted out of it—what *do* I want, anyway?

They went into the house, still without a word. Donna sat down in the nearest chair, close to tears.

Caldwell stood there looking at her with combined fury and sadness. "You really are something," he said. "Why the hell did you bring him there in the first place? You could have just thrown a hand grenade into the club. It would have been quicker."

"Leave me alone," Donna muttered.

"Are you proud of yourself?" Why couldn't he

offer her something besides anger? He loved her, but how could he show it, other than trying to set her on the right road as well as he knew how? "Are you?" he repeated.

"Why don't you ask yourself that question?" Donna flashed out.

Her father stared down at her. "What the hell do you mean by that?"

"You set the whole thing up, not me," she told him.

"I don't know what the hell you're talking about," he snapped.

Donna was fighting tears. Her anger helped. "Captain Gordon," she said. "Who I can see, who I can't see. You probably have it all written out in one of your stupid folders. You don't ask me what I want—you tell me what you want. I never enlisted in your Army, Colonel. This is *my* life. *I* decide what I want."

"And you've sure done a wonderful job of it."

"Well, I never got any help from you!" she yelped. "All I ever got were rules—your rules. You decided what was fair, what was foul."

Caldwell was stung to the quick. He covered by looking around for a cigar. "This is ridiculous," he managed to say.

"Don't you turn away from me!" Donna shouted at him.

"I'm not going to listen to any more of this," he told her calmly. One thing he did know, and that was how to keep control of a situation. Well, it worked with the Vietcong and it worked with soldiers under his command, but it didn't seem to work nearly so well with his kid.

"That's perfect," Donna said scornfully. "You're done talking, so there's nothing more to say. You're a—a coward!"

"That's enough!" he told her. He walked away. Keeping his temper. Looking for a goddamned cigar, where the hell were they?

She was up out of the chair and following him. "No, it's not!" she persisted. "It's never been enough!"

He walked through the front hall, into the dining room. She was right on his heels.

"What are you afraid of?" she asked.

Caldwell kept on storming around, opening drawers and pushing aside piles of papers, looking for the goddamned cigars that had been right in plain sight a couple of hours ago. He felt trapped, frustrated. She stayed right behind him, practically standing on his heels.

"Just tell me so I know," she insisted.

He started looking around like a trapped animal, checking for escape routes. Maybe he left the goddamned things in the kitchen . . .

"You think I'm like her? Is that it?" Donna asked shrilly.

"Stop it," Caldwell told her.

"You turned your back on her, too, didn't you?" she went on. "That's why she did it. It was your fault, wasn't it? Wasn't it, you . . . you bastard!"

Caldwell wheeled around. His hand was in the air, ready to strike her. It froze. For a second, they stood there face to face, his hand open and poised.

"Do it!" Donna said. "Do it!"

Caldwell didn't move.

She turned and walked out of the house. He stood there for a long time, letting his hand drop slowly back to his side.

He heard her car start up with a heavy rev and then she was gone. Caldwell looked around the empty kitchen. Empty house. How the hell were you supposed to know these things . . . he opened a cabinet and took down a bottle of Scotch whiskey. He didn't bother with a glass.

A couple of hours later, he decided it wasn't such a hot idea to drink alone, after all. Company was what he needed. An old pal to tell his troubles to. He had an old pal. He had the best old pal anybody ever had. How he managed to drive to Maclure's apartment building is anybody's guess, but he got there in one piece and as far as he knew, no damage done. He decided the intelligent thing to do was to climb up the fire escape. It seemed like a very intelligent thing to do. There it was, just begging to be climbed. So he did.

It was only a four-story building, but he had a hell of a time scaling the damned thing. The lights from the skyscraping Trans Am building were glaring in his eyes, and he had to hang on to the liquor bottle with one hand and the whole damned fire escape was rattling against the brick side of the building as his weight made it sway. Or seem to sway. Whichever.

Perilously, he maneuvered himself up and up without anything important crashing down to the alleyway below. He finally reached the window he had in mind. He sat down and started pounding on the glass pane.

After a minute or so the window slid up. A hand came out, steady as a rock, pointing a pearl-handled .45 right between Caldwell's eyes. Caldwell grinned and leaned against the muzzle of the gun. It didn't budge an inch.

"Hey, Top," Caldwell said loudly.

The rest of the arm came out of the window and with it Maclure's friendly white head. "Jesus, Colonel. What the hell are you doing?"

Caldwell considered for a moment. The .45 had withdrawn, giving him nothing to lean against.

"I'm getting drunk," he finally announced. "That's what. Why, what does it look like to you I'm doing?"

"It looks like you've already done that," Maclure said.

"I want to get drunker," Caldwell told him. He looked up. "I'm going up to your roof," he said. He started to pull himself up but the iron rungs of the fire escape seemed to have him caught.

"Why?" Maclure asked, reasonably.

"Because this fire escape hurts my ass," Caldwell explained. He tried again to get to his feet. One foot kept getting twisted under him. Complicated.

"Why don't you come inside?" Maclure suggested. He was trying to keep the conversation down a few decibels, but Caldwell didn't seem to know or care that it was the dead of night and people around there might be sleeping, or trying to.

"Because," Caldwell said loudly. "Because I'm outside, that's why I can't come inside. Come on outside. Come on up to the roof with me."

"You know what time it is?"

"Who cares?"

Maclure considered this, shrugged and said, "I sure as shit don't." With that he climbed through the window and joined Caldwell on the fire escape.

The obstacle course presented by the narrow ladder skimming up the last story to the roof was no more difficult than a basic-training problem. Of course being drunk didn't help, and having a few years between you and basic training didn't help, but the ex-sergeant had assisted the colonel over a few obstacles before, and one way or another, they made it.

Caldwell, heaved over the parapet from behind, tumbled easily onto the tarpaper-covered roof. By the time Maclure came alongside, Caldwell had found himself a low brick ledge to lean against. He was sitting quite comfortably, legs sprawled out before him, back against the bricks. Maclure, in a plaid flannel bathrobe over his skivvies, sat down alongside. He reached for the bottle that Caldwell still clutched in one hand.

"Here, pal," Caldwell said genially, handing it over.

Maclure held the bottle up in the light of the Trans Am building. There wasn't much left. "Drink this all by yourself?" he asked.

Caldwell nodded. "Yeah. You can keep that one," he added generously. He reached into the inside pocket of his jacket and produced another bottle, this one full.

Maclure took a long swig of Scotch. "Whoa. Oh, boy!" It was strong stuff. It had been a long time since he had swilled Scotch down straight like that.

"I've lost her," Caldwell said.

"Who?" Maclure asked. He took another long tuck in the supply. "Oh, my!" he muttered as it went down all fire and brimstone.

"Donna," Caldwell said sadly.

Maclure thought this over, then he shook his head with absolute conviction. "Naw, you didn't lose her," he said. "She's just grown up. You got to start to accept that."

Caldwell stared at the fresh bottle in his hand. He broke the seal and twisted the cap open. "She hates me," he told his friend. Then he took a long drink.

Maclure tried shaking his head and swallowing at the same time. Then he leaned back against the bricks and tried to see some stars beyond the city lights. He thought about his talk with Donna, and he knew he was right when he said, gently, "She doesn't hate you. She's just trying to measure up to you. Sometimes that ain't easy," he added.

Caldwell looked at Maclure, trying to get him in focus. Maclure's plaid bathrobe was cozy, his bare legs comical, his white hair hard to believe, and his face the greatest comfort in Caldwell's life. His only friend. He would listen to Maclure. Maclure had saved his life. He wouldn't bullshit now.

"You kinda want perfection in people," Maclure was saying. "There's not a lot of perfect people around, though."

Caldwell nodded thoughtfully. Then he took another drink from the full bottle. "You know I love her, don't you?"

"Of course I know," Maclure told him. He reached for the bottle. "It ain't important what I know," he said. "It's important what she knows. When's the last time you told her that?"

Caldwell didn't answer.

"Ya see?" Maclure said. He took a long swallow and passed the bottle back.

"She knows I love her," Caldwell protested.

Maclure shook his head. "I've known buildings that are easier to talk to than you."

Caldwell sighed and looked down at his feet, splayed out funny on the tarpaper. He never sprawled, and here he was, sprawling. He must be drunk. He looked at Maclure's bare legs too. He thought of the two of them in a jungle somewhere.

"Hey!" he said suddenly. "Was that my gun you pointed at me?"

Maclure nodded sheepishly. "Yeah. I took it out of the museum," he said.

"Why?"

"I just wanted to hold on to it for a while."

"Huh? What for?" Caldwell asked.

Maclure shrugged. "I had my reasons. Give me some of that." He reached out his hand and Caldwell gave him the bottle again. Maclure took a large hit.

"You know," he said, "sometimes I think it was a lot easier winning that medal than wearing it." He looked around at the skyline. "You think any of the people over there give a shit about us?" he asked. The Scotch was getting to him and it felt pretty good. What the hell.

Caldwell followed Maclure's glance across the sleeping city. He shrugged. "*We* give a shit about them," he said.

He took a drink. "You know what I think?" He didn't wait for Maclure to answer. "America is like a big fancy house," he said, a drunken philosopher who sometimes makes good sense. "And we are the Doberman pinschers. When a guy hears a noise downstairs, he's really happy to have his big ugly dog, right? But the next day he's got friends coming over for lunch, he locks up the dog. Why? Because he's embarrassed."

Maclure was listening; he nodded.

"But," Caldwell went on, "that night, he sure as shit unlocks that dog, so his fancy house is protected. Oh, and if someone breaks in and the dog doesn't bite his ass, then he's gonna take a rolled up newspaper, and smack him right in the fuckin' mouth. It's like that," he said solemnly.

Maclure nodded. The Scotch was passing between them like a birdie in a badminton match. Caldwell belched loudly.

"I remember like it was yesterday," he said. "I was ten. My old man was laid off . . . again. He told us we're leaving Edinburgh, and we're going to America. He gave me this book about Thomas Jefferson, and I read it right through."

They sat in silence for a companionable moment.

Then Caldwell went on, "Next thing I know, I'm standing on the deck of this ship. My old man yells, 'Look, there she is!' I could just see over the railing. Well!!! Her look and the green color of her face . . . you know! She really is that beautiful. I just started to cry. Imagine. Me!"

They drank on it.

"It's like you've been born blind," Caldwell went on, "and then somebody comes up with a new kind of operation . . . and suddenly you get your sight. And you see things different from someone who's never been blind. I think maybe you see more. Anyway . . . that's the way I feel about America, and that's why I'm a soldier."

He took a long thirsty drink.

"So nobody has to thank us. It's really not important," he said. He looked at the bottle in his hand. "Maclure," he said, "I'm really drunk."

Maclure knew just what he meant. "As a skunk," he agreed.

Caldwell nodded and then closed his eyes. That was it for the night. With memories of having done this before, years before, under worse conditions, Maclure figured he could do it again. He bent down and scooped the colonel up onto his shoulder, fireman's carry. The colonel had put on a couple of pounds since 'Nam, and the sarge a few years. But he managed. He just hoped the door to the roof was unlocked, because the ladder down to the fire escape and the window might be almost as rough as jungle terrain, although nobody was shooting at them this time.

He used Caldwell's inert boots to kick against the door; it gave. Maclure grunted with relief and made his way carefully down the stairs to his apartment. He laid his burden down on the couch. Straightening up, he saw the .45 lying on the end table. He picked it up and put it in his bathrobe pocket.

Maclure was a man accustomed to living alone. He talked out loud sometimes when there wasn't anybody in particular there to talk to. It was just a habit, nothing serious. He didn't do it in public, just sometimes to fill up the empty space in his quarters. He did it now, without thinking. "Funny," he said, looking down at Caldwell's inert body, "how five minutes one way or the other can make such a difference."

Not expecting an answer, he started to turn away, back to bed himself. But Caldwell was not completely out. "Five minutes?" he muttered drowsily. He didn't bother to open his eyes.

"Yeah," Maclure explained, from the doorway of his bedroom, "if I'd been five minutes earlier, or five minutes later, I might not have found you in the jungle."

"Oh," Caldwell grunted.

"And . . . if Patti Jean Lynch had been five minutes earlier . . . or five minutes later . . ."

He trailed off, went into his bedroom, and opened the closet door. He reached up onto the neat shelf and pulled down an olive drab blanket labeled "U.S. Army." He brought it back into the living room. ". . . maybe none of this would have happened," he concluded. But this time Caldwell was off and snoring quietly. The old sergeant major put the blanket over him, gently. He took a cushion from the end of the couch and cradled it under the colonel's head.

Then he hit the sack himself.

CHAPTER 15

She heard music playing inside Austin's apartment. When Donna knocked at his door, she didn't know whether he would welcome her or throw some totally deserved sneers at her and slam it in her face. She felt so small she was kind of surprised he could actually see her. He looked kind of stunned when he opened the door. To her immense relief, he gestured for her to come in.

"I'm sorry," she blurted. "Truly sorry. I acted like a real bitch, and . . . I don't want to act that way with you."

"Sit down, you want a drink?" he asked.

She shook her head, no.

"Coffee?"

That sounded good. "Yes, please."

It was already made. He had been having some himself and he just grabbed another mug from the kitchen and brought it out, hot and black and steamy. He handed it to her and sat on a footstool, facing her, waiting.

"I . . . I just had a fight with my dad," she told him. Maddeningly, she was close to tears. She didn't have any way of knowing that showing a bit of vulnerability just now was the way to open his door again. He didn't want to believe she was all hard and tough Army brat. He just looked at her, not without sympathy, but waiting for her to get it all out.

"Well, anyway . . ." She fumbled for words. She took a sip of coffee. "Hey, you put sugar in it, just the right amount!"

"Good memory," he said, tapping the side of his temple. But he wasn't smiling, and it was still all going to be up to her.

"I got scared . . . oh, he'd never hurt me, not intentionally, not physically or anything, I mean. But . . . the look on his face—he was scared! I've never seen that before. My whole life, he taught me not to say too much, not to show too much, never to lose control."

Austin was listening carefully. He nodded, looking like he understood. Donna felt better and began to talk more freely. "It works, you know," she told him. "Nobody can hurt you if you never let anybody in."

"Yeah, I know," Austin said.

"I have to give him credit," Donna went on. "He taught me well. He even tries to keep me out. He *does* keep me out. That hurts. And . . . that's what I've been doing to you."

"Go on," Austin said.

"I've been trying not to lose control. It's lonely. I'd . . . I'd sleep with you, as long as it was on my terms." She paused, a little shaky, and took a long drink of the coffee. They both knew she had never been able to talk this way before, not to anyone, ever. She wasn't even sure why it was so important now to open up—to someone—before she got as rocklike as her father. To someone? Anyone? Or in fact only to Jay Austin? She didn't know, but it felt like fresh air was coming into her lungs and whatever was happening to her heart was healthy and good. She was trusting him.

"I was doing okay," she said. "I really was. But then . . . the more time I spent with you, the scarier it got. That's why I behaved that way at the Officers' Club. I couldn't run away from you anymore . . . so . . . I guess I wanted you to run away from me."

He didn't say anything. He was looking at her with understanding and . . . maybe it was love. Anyway, he didn't have to say anything.

"I don't want to hurt you like that anymore," she said simply. "I love you."

Now suddenly the tears that had been standing in her eyes spilled over. She looked straight into Austin's eyes, her chin unconsciously jutting up like her father's did when he was standing off a possible threat. Through the tears, Donna smiled.

The sudden overflow in his own heart propelled Austin forward. He took her in his arms and held her tightly. She cried for a minute or two while he held her. When they kissed, her mouth was sweet and salty, and then, of course, so was his.

The next morning, Austin pulled up in front of the Caldwell house at eight-forty. Caldwell was waiting for him on the porch. As he came down the walk toward the car, Austin observed that he looked like he hadn't slept much. He was dressed in fatigues, making him look a little more human than the brass suit with all the medals did. He was rumpled, his hair still damp from a shower. His eyes were little slits. When he got into Austin's car and slammed the door, the noise of it pained him visibly. Oh, ho, a hangover, and it's a doozy, Austin observed silently. I'll bet his teeth itch. I know the feeling. I'll go easy on him. I have nothing but generous feelings toward this man this morning.

"You're ten minutes late," Caldwell snapped as he settled himself in the passenger seat.

Motor running, hands on the wheel, Austin decided they'd better say it all now, before they started out. "I've got some good news and some bad news," he told the colonel.

The colonel weighed this. "What's the good news," he grunted.

"Donna's with me," Austin told him. He steeled himself for the explosion, although Caldwell's delicate condition this morning might preclude anything noisy.

The colonel just stared out the window at the blue morning sky. He peered upward from under the brim of his camouflage cap. Wisps of fog were drifting out to sea. In the distance you could hear squad leaders shouting orders: "Owwwwt—*face*" and "Leeeeeeeffffft *hup!*" wafted on the breeze that rustled the leaves on this otherwise still autumn day.

Finally Caldwell spoke, still gazing out the window and up into the blue, his eyes hardly visible at all. "That's the good news?" he said, acid in his tone.

"The bad news is that I love her," Austin said quickly.

Caldwell nodded. The fight had gone out of him. "So do I," he said so softly Austin could hardly catch it.

"Tennnnnnn—*hup!*" far in the distance.

Caldwell turned his eyes right, looking straight out in front of him. "Look, are we going to sit here discussing my personal life all morning?" he snapped.

"Nope," Austin said. He revved up the gas pedal. He cleared his throat. Then he said, "The car that killed Lawrence is registered to George Spota."

"Arthur Peale owns Black Mountain Water," Caldwell came right back at him.

Their eyes met briefly, finally, as each quickly digested the fruit of the other's research. Austin nodded. He slammed the car into gear. Tires burned and they were gone.

He pulled up at a deli and Caldwell got out, came back in a couple of minutes with a styro cup of coffee. He didn't take the lid off till they got to the Black Mountain Water building. This time he let Austin go in alone. He sipped at the coffee as if it were medicine, which in this case it was. He watched the delivery trucks pulling out of the lot. One by one, the drivers came out of the dispatching office and picked up their rigs at the loading dock. They spun out of there irregularly and Caldwell was mildly amused, after a few minutes, to see Austin racing across the lot, dodging the trucks with a zigzag running style. He piled back into the Dodge.

"Spota's in the third truck from the end," he said, gasping for breath. They watched the loading dock. When the third truck from the end left the gate, the Dodge was not far behind.

They ducked and weaved a bit, but the heavy rush-hour traffic let them follow without being obvious about it. The white truck with the huge black mountain painted on its sides and rear was plotting a steady course. Spota maneuvered through the commercial streets to Third, stayed on Third east all the way to the broad traverse of the Embarcadero. Trucks and heavy commercial traffic moved along the waterfront drive in good order, occasionally dropping off in a right turn onto one of the loading docks that lined the picturesque working port. Ships plying all the exotic ports of the Pacific were lined up along the embarkation docks that jutted out into the Bay.

The very name of the Embarcadero sounds romantic and compelling to anyone with an adventurous spirit. Austin drove and walked this way frequently but his excitement for it had never diminished. He kept his eye on the truck ahead but still he had time to savor the vitality and contrasts of the historic seaport. He drove past huge sheds in which were stored, temporarily, pillage from the Far East—well, not pillage any more, but fair trade: automobiles, tubs of soy, cases of tea and barrels of porcelain, art objects and cheap toys, clothing and jewels and spices and silks—and the stuff of American designers, too, made in Korea or Japan or Taiwan. The smells of the waterfront were sensuous invitations to hop a ship and follow your nose: perfume and rice wine mixed with diesel fuel; the stench of animal hides vied with pungent sauces and all were tinged with the salty tang of fish and gulls and the sea itself. As they passed the *Oriana*'s pier, they saw that she was about to set out on a cruise—paper streamers fluttered and music could be heard and the shouts and laughter of people on deck, people left behind waving—all fueled with ritual champagne despite the early hour.

They passed the Ferry Building, and Pier 23 where you can still go to hear great jazz, and the Eagle Cafe where the last of the real old salts sit over coffee and talk about the days when they shipped out under sail. Pier 37 with the eclectic restaurant called the Crow's Nest. Behind and beyond all the buildings and cranes lifting cargo containers were the high red and white and black funnels of the ships pawing impatiently at their lines, waiting to be off again.

"He's taking the Travis Boulevard off-ramp," Caldwell said.

"I see him." Austin shut his mind to his romantic daydreams. He always loved the Embarcadero, but he wasn't usually this poetic about it all; might have something to do with the fact that he was in love . . . "I'd like to get you on a slow boat to China,"—that was a song lyric he had heard once, it had been the soundtrack in his head the whole while he drove the waterfront just now. He was even thinking honeymoon; how would the colonel feel about that, he wondered wildly. He moved to the right-turn lane and took the ramp himself. The truck led them to the main gate of Travis Air Force Base. There were two lanes going in and two coming out. A guard post in the center was manned by Air Force security. In the far right lane, the water truck slowed, was waved on in, and went straight through.

Austin slowed the Dodge. They watched the truck disappear into the base. He turned to Caldwell. "Any suggestions?"

Caldwell pointed straight ahead, to the gate. "Go on," he said.

Austin shrugged and cruised up to the guard post. He rolled down his window and came to a stop as a sharp young corporal stepped out. Caldwell pulled out his wallet and flashed an ID at him. The guard saluted.

"Morning, sir," he said. Caldwell returned the salute. "Destination?" the guard asked.

Caldwell leaned forward, trying not to wince from the sudden pain that hit him in the hangover. "MAC terminal," he said sharply. "I'm catching a hop to Hawaii and I'm late."

"Yes, sir," the guard snapped. He stepped back and reached into the window of the post station. Austin grinned at Caldwell, impressed. Caldwell shrugged. The guard handed Austin a pass, and they rolled on through the gate like milk through a baby.

They caught sight of the Black Mountain Water truck about a half mile ahead, following the main road that cut past the airfield's most serious buildings. The thunderous sounds of C-5s, C-141s, and civilian charter cargo planes taking off and whining to a landing halt caromed around them on both sides. The main road went past the control tower, and then the passenger terminal, where civilian crews worked both inside the building and out on the tarmac. The maintenance buildings and support facilities were all adjacent to the airfield. The water truck turned off at the entry road to the support facility.

Austin stopped the Dodge nearby, pulled up to the curb. There were enough people moving around the general area so that they didn't look at all conspicuous when they got out of the car and stood eyeballing the action over at the supply building. The water truck was parked in front of the place. A husky, beer-bellied, fortyish man got out of the truck and went around to unload two hefty bottles of water crated with wooden slats. With a mighty heave, he hoisted them onto his shoulders and headed for the door of the building. He set one crated bottle down outside the door, used his free hand to open the latch, and went in carrying the other bottle.

"Recognize him?" Austin asked. "Is that Spota?"

"Yeah. That's him. Used to be Sergeant Spota."

Austin nodded. "Right in front of God and everybody," he commented.

Caldwell nodded, although it hurt his head. "That's the most successful way," he said. "None of that covert shit."

They took off at the same instant to follow Spota into the support facility.

As they neared the building, Austin saw a crew van pull up ahead of them, up to the door. He stopped in his tracks, and elbowed Caldwell, who stopped too. They watched the van, which was most likely returning from a civilian charter plane. The thing that was so interesting about it was that right behind the two men who got out of the van, another man in maintenance overalls emerged, carrying a bottle of Black Mountain water.

They watched with great interest as the maintenance man deposited the bottle on a pallet just outside the door, then entered the terminal. The other two men had stayed with the van, almost, you might think, guarding it.

Caldwell and Austin walked over to the van. They looked inside at the perfectly normal-looking flight crew.

"Excuse me, Captain," Caldwell said to the clean-cut young Viking in the pilot's uniform. "Where did you come in from?" He made it sound official.

"Clark," the pilot said.

Caldwell frowned. "Philippines?" he asked.

The pilot was annoyed. "You know another Clark Air Force Base, Colonel?"

Austin was keeping an eye on the door of the supply building. It opened and Spota came out, minus the bottle. He strode toward his truck, and Austin got fidgety. "Come on," he muttered to Caldwell. But the colonel seemed to have plenty of time to hang around gabbing. Austin pulled at his arm, and Caldwell stepped out of hearing range of the crew in the van.

"He's going back to his truck," he said urgently. "We're going to lose him if we don't move it."

"Right," Caldwell said. They headed for the Dodge.

"What's with the Philippines?" Austin asked as they hustled themselves into the car. The truck was rounding into the main street of the base.

"I don't know," Caldwell said. "But something."

The rest of the morning was uninspired. Following a water delivery truck on its rounds, even in the scenic Bay Area, is not fascinating. And when the guy with you is worried about his daughter, whom you left all snuggled sweetly in your bed, and he's got a jumbo-sized hangover to make him a bit jumpy in general, things can get a little tedious. Austin counted twelve stops in Vallejo, and fourteen more in Novato, which was another fifteen miles west. The Dodge stuck to the delivery truck like it was on a rubber leash.

Spota had his lunch at a little Mexican place off the road between nowhere and more of the same. Caldwell and Austin survived on lemonade bought from two seven-year-old kids at a homemade stand while waiting for the only traffic light in Lakeville to change.

By the time Spota achieved the slow completion of his appointed rounds, late-afternoon sun slanted through the trees. Winding back to the city, with the Dodge still on his tail, he approached the Presidio from the north. Caldwell couldn't suppress a sigh of relief as they entered the grassy, tree-shaded avenues; the military orderliness provided an ironic ambience of tranquillity and peace. They followed the truck to the Officers'

Club. Spota was making his final delivery of the day.

"Take this turn," Caldwell said as soon as they saw where the truck was headed. "We can get a good look without him spotting us."

Austin turned and climbed a hill behind the club. The opaque reds and oranges of the lowered sun turned the ancient adobe walls of the building to burnt sugar. He stopped the car just at the crest of the hill. He got out of the car and joined Caldwell. They watched keenly as Spota got out of his truck, went around to pick up the last remaining bottle from his load. He hoisted it and went inside the club.

Caldwell lifted his fatigue cap and rubbed his forehead. He had been puzzling over something all day; now it came tumbling out. "Why water from the Philippines?" he wondered.

Austin nodded. He had been thinking along the same lines. "Something's in that bottle besides water."

"Right." Caldwell nodded vigorously. At least the hangover was finally gone. He'd never drink like that again. "And it's something worth killing for."

They stared down at the empty truck, the rear door to the Officers' Club, the mostly empty parking lot.

"It comes from the Philippines," Caldwell mused aloud, "and it's delivered to Spota. Then Spota delivers it to the bottling company."

"Looks that way, and then . . ." Austin trailed off. It didn't account for what had gone wrong.

"Except . . . he must have made a mistake," Caldwell said. "He left the wrong bottle in the Officers' Club. That night . . . he retraced his steps and came back here."

"And Patti Jean surprised him . . . and he smoked her," Austin finished sadly.

"I want to know what's in that bottle," the colonel said.

"Right." Austin looked over at Caldwell, who was still frowning hard, still trying to fit some pieces together. "What's with you?" he asked the colonel.

"Something's missing," Caldwell said. "Something about the Philippines. There's another hand in this."

Just then Spota came out of the club and headed for his truck. Austin and Caldwell got back in the car, headed down the other side of the hill, and caught up with him as he headed for the Mountain Lake exit.

The truck homed south and east, winding through city streets to the Black Mountain Water Company. Spota went through the gate into the parking area. Austin parked across the street.

"I'll call backup," he told Caldwell. He reached for the car phone.

Caldwell was deep in thought. "There's a goddamned piece missing," he said.

Austin couldn't figure what was bugging the old man. It seemed pretty complete to him. "What are you talking about?" he asked with minor irritation. He was looking forward to getting home. He flashed on his last sight of Donna's tousled yellow curls on his pillow. He shook himself back to duty, and laid out the scam as he had it put together. "Lawrence and Peale knew each other in 'Nam," he said. "Spota's another crony. So what's missing?"

They watched a brown Mustang enter the parking area in front of the water company.

"Shit," Caldwell said under his breath.

They watched as a white-haired man, of stocky

build, about five-ten, got out of the Mustang and headed for the front entrance of the building. It was Maclure.

Austin didn't want to look at Caldwell's face. Maclure was his best buddy. The guy who had made Medal of Honor for saving Caldwell's ass. The colonel's granite chin was in danger of crumbling and Austin didn't particularly want to be a witness.

"Oh, shit," he echoed, from the heart.

Caldwell pulled himself together fast. "Of course," he said in a voice that emotion couldn't get into with a red-hot wedge, "Maclure served with Lawrence in Vietnam, too." His voice cracked, just a moment's betrayal. He cleared his throat and went on in a dead monotone. "They'd need him, or somebody like him, to set it up. He knows every maintenance man in the Far East."

Austin looked at him. Caldwell was hanging tough. "Okay," he said. "Let's get 'em."

CHAPTER 16

THE CAFETERIA OF the Officers' Club at this hour was bleak and dull, except for the extraordinary glitter of a small mountain of diamonds that had just been poured onto a black velvet cloth on one of the tables. Three men stood admiring the cache that Spota had just removed from its hidden colander inside the large-necked bottle.

Arthur Peale was grinning like a greedy pig at feeding time. He was still in suit and tie, looking exactly as he had in his office the day before—cool and calm and in control. He was holding an empty duffel bag. Right at his side was his yuppie assistant, Mark Wallach, whose twitching nose betrayed that he was just a smidge out of control. The third guy was the same maintenance man who had gotten out of the crew van at Travis AFB. He was still in his overalls.

Peale took a jeweler's magnifier out of his pocket, held it over the sparklers, and took a close, careful look. He straightened up. "These are good quality," he told the maintenance jockey, whose smile got wider than before. "You can cable our friend in Manila and tell him he's done well."

"You can also tell him he's out of work, 'cause this shit is going to stop right now."

The four men whirled to see Maclure standing in the doorway leading to the kitchen. He was alone.

Arthur Peale, after an instant's unease, was smiling again. "What are you doing here?" he asked Maclure pleasantly. But next to him, his gofer Mark slid his hand into his well-cut sports jacket pocket.

"You told me nobody would get hurt," Maclure said.

Peale nodded. "Nobody was supposed to get hurt," he agreed. His voicebox sounded like it had been dipped in Mrs. Butterworth's syrup.

"Tell that to the girl Lawrence killed," Maclure said sharply.

Mark Wallach gripped the handle of his gun but didn't take it out of his pocket. Not yet.

"Don't worry about it. Lawrence has been dealt with," Peale assured Maclure.

The old sergeant stood his ground. "That's not enough, pal," he said. "I'm telling you that it's over."

"It's a little late for conscience, don't you think?" Peale said.

"It's over," Maclure repeated stubbornly. "I'm blowing the whistle."

"Who the hell do you think you are?" Mark blurted out.

Maclure stood his ground. "I'm the infantry, sonny," he answered.

"The war's been over for a long time, old man. Nobody cares. Go back to your silly museum and play with your medals." The snip seemed proud of himself for that; he almost wagged his tail and looked up to his master for a pat on the head.

Peale stood quietly, just listening.

Maclure was turning furious. "You open your mouth one more time," he told Mark clearly, "and I'm going to shove your head so far up your ass you'll be talking out of your armpit."

And outside the club, up on the hill, Austin and Caldwell seemed to be a study in arrested motion, still sitting in the Dodge. Austin was ready to barrel down there, bust into the place, and snare whoever was doing whatever. But Caldwell was strangely quiet. Paralyzed, almost. He just sat and stared out of the windshield down at the parking lot of the club, now bathed in the soft twilight.

"Caldwell?"

Austin was impatient and getting pissed off, but still he couldn't help feeling for the guy. First the fight with Donna. Then he tied one on and ended up with nothing but a monumental hangover. Driving around all day following a goddamned delivery truck out in the sticks, in the company of a fellow he wasn't really too nuts about in general. And then . . . a real last straw, his best buddy turns out to be what's wrong with the whole picture . . .

Suddenly Caldwell pounded the dashboard, hard, with his fist. "Goddamn son of a *bitch!*" he yowled.

Thunderstruck, Austin could only just sit and watch.

It seemed to take forever, and more cussing than Austin had heard even when he was in the Army himself, but finally Caldwell got control. His expression then could have shattered glass.

Without a word, Caldwell opened the car door and piled out. He left it open, and didn't turn back to see if Austin was coming along. He strode down that hillside like the Four Hundred moving in on the Valley of Death. Austin had to scramble to catch up.

Inside, Peale took a step toward Maclure. "This is ridiculous. I'm sure we can find a solution. Look, Sergeant, we're already sorry about what happened. Believe me, it was the last thing I wanted. However . . . it's done. There's nothing we can do about it now, is there?"

"I don't think you hear so good," Maclure told him. "I said it's over."

He pulled out a pearl-handled .45 and pointed it at Peale, who stopped in his tracks.

"But what do you think you're accomplishing?" Peale asked reasonably.

"I'm going to make things right," Maclure answered.

At the same time, Austin, following Caldwell around to the front of the club, pulled a leather case from his pocket. He chose a tool, and when they got to the door he started working on picking the lock. But Caldwell was like a crazed animal. He wanted to get inside, and he wanted it badly, really badly. He backed off and primed himself to kick the door in.

Austin dropped his pick. "You want to set off the goddamn alarm?" he hissed in a furious whisper. He took the gun from his holster and handed it to the colonel, whose camouflage fatigues weren't designed for carrying arms. "Here, you're gonna need this," he said. "You'll get your ass shot off if you go in there that mad," he added.

"Okay! You gonna open it?!!" Caldwell didn't bother to keep his voice down.

Inside, Mark Wallach was saying, with a sneer, "He wants more money."

"I don't like you," Maclure told him. He looked back at Arthur Peale. "Tell him I don't like him," he said.

Outside, Austin was still working on the lock. Caldwell was snorting and pacing and growling like a caged panther. "Come on, come on, open it!" he yowled.

"Say that one more time and I'll shoot you," Austin warned him.

Inside, Peale was still trying to act reasonable. "I know you never wanted to be a part of this," he was saying to Maclure. "I know you're a man of honor. Lawrence had something on you, didn't he, something going back to the days in Vietnam, something to do with the black market? You made one mistake, a long time ago . . . and you didn't want your name destroyed . . . so you agreed to look the other way. I'm right, aren't I?"

Maclure didn't answer. But he didn't stop the swiftie from spelling it out, either. Maybe he needed to hear it. Maybe he was just letting the joker have his last words. He let him go on.

"I sympathize with you," Peale said, oozing snake oil. "But there's no reason to ruin everything now . . . and your name along with it. You'd hurt yourself as much as everybody else."

He was finished. Maclure answered in the same patient, deadly calm tone he had used since he walked in. "I don't give a shit about myself any more," he said flatly. "I'm going to make things right."

Maclure never saw the blow that hit him in the back of the head. He went sprawling on the floor. The pearl-handled .45 skittered and clattered on the tiles before it spun to a halt. Mark Wallach had taken his hand out of his pocket and his small automatic pistol with it. He glanced quickly at

Peale, who nodded his approval. The so-called maintenance man walked swiftly over to Maclure.

Even for Austin, picking the lock was a slow business; it took delicacy and skill. But suddenly Caldwell had no more patience. He pushed Austin aside and kicked in the door, all with one flowing motion like a choreographed dancer. A shrill alarm immediately screamed, loud enough to be heard a mile away. Caldwell charged into the dark entryway of the club. Stopping only to draw his spare .32 from the leg holster, Austin followed him inside.

The alarm had sent everybody into an instant panic.

"Somebody's inside!" Peale shouted. "Let's get out of here!"

He started shoving diamonds into his pockets, no time for opening the duffel. Spota and the man in overalls helped him clear the table, loading their own pockets with the sparkling stones. They dashed out of the cafeteria. The alarm screeched deafeningly.

Caldwell dashed through the bar, across the dance floor, and off under an EXIT sign on the left. Right behind him, Austin exploded through the room and took the exit on the right.

He found a closed door. He kicked it open, pistol cocked, but it only led into a hallway. He went in, and the door closed behind him.

A double door with glass windows led to the cafeteria. Austin pushed the doors open and burst in, at the same moment that Caldwell entered from the other side. Plastic chairs and formica tables clashed with the three-hundred-year-old composition of the walls. Austin flicked a switch and harsh fluorescent light glistened off a Black Mountain Water bottle, still in its crate, but with the top off. It sat near a table on which were scattered some glittering stones that caught the light.

Caldwell got to the table first. He picked up one of the diamonds, looked at it and puckered up his lips in a silent, appreciative whistle. Austin took a look and nodded.

The alarm kept on shrieking. Cautiously, Caldwell and Austin moved out of the cafeteria, into the rear hallway. Nothing. The storeroom where Patti Jean had been killed was undisturbed. The rear door was ajar; in their haste to get out, the diamond smugglers—and Maclure—hadn't bothered to shut it. No sign of anyone in the parking lot now. All was quiet except for the alarm, which blared on and on and on.

Austin and Caldwell raced up the hill and piled into the Dodge. Austin turned on the siren as soon as he left the Presidio and hit the city streets. They took corners on two wheels and took hills like they were lying down, and reached the Black Mountain Water Company in mere minutes.

They set off the alarm here, too. Kicking the door in, they found the reception area empty. Gloria was off somewhere enjoying her Saturday, probably at a rock concert.

The explosion felt like it might have been a grenade, lobbed close enough to shatter the front window of the building. Glass hailed in on them as Austin and Caldwell hit the floor. They didn't hang around, but crawled quickly on their bellies through a door out into a hallway. In the relative safety of the enclosed space, they scrambled, but fast, to their feet.

Caldwell turned right and Austin took the left. They ran through the hall, weapons ready and adrenaline pumping through their veins.

There was a flight of stairs at the end of Austin's route; he took them three at a time. At the top he peered through a Judas-hole into the huge heart of the bottling plant. All was still, the giant machinery halted for the weekend. He was on the second level, above the working floor where a series of catwalks crossed over the plant. Silently, slowly, Austin pushed the door open with his foot, checking all directions with his eye and his gun. The assembly plant was a cavernous room, about the size of a large hangar. Rays of the setting sun poured through skylights on the high ceiling, glinting off the steel equipment. Rows of empty bottles stood on a wide conveyor belt that snaked around and up and down through the heavy complex machinery like a roller-coaster track.

On the level where he stood, the catwalk continued around the entire perimeter of the room, with crosswalks as well, for servicing the huge pieces of equipment. Two glass control shacks sat on opposite walls, abutting where he stood. Near one of them, about twenty yards away, two figures stood on the walkway, peering down into the maze of silent machinery, searching for something—or someone. Nothing moved. The alarm went on wailing.

Then something down there did move. Austin caught it in the corner of his eye. He wheeled around, gun first, pressed himself against the shadows along the wall and peered down. He held the .32 ready. Then it moved again: it was Caldwell, inching very cautiously, squeezing along behind some machinery. Austin stayed quiet, covering him. By instinct or experience or jungle guts—they both knew the drill. It didn't matter how you knew, it was what you knew and how much you could count on yourself and your buddy to do it when the time came. Danger smelled like your own blood tasted—pungent, sharp, and very, very real.

Caldwell was trying to move and stay hidden, too, but it wasn't working, because all of a sudden there was one hell of a blast from an automatic, setting off a wild shower of sparks as bullets bounced off the heavy steel machinery inches from his head. Trying to see where it was coming from, he moved again, but hardly at all. *Uh-Uh-Uh-Uh-Uh*—another deadly burst of fire and sparks narrowly missed him.

"Up there!" Austin yelled. Caldwell looked up at Austin, followed his pointing and saw the two men on the catwalk near the skylight.

Austin's shout had momentarily distracted the shooter's attention, giving Caldwell a half second to look and leap at the same time. Now he was blocked by a big instrument and had no way around it. He pressed against it, trying to find an angle. The two men who had the bead on him waited for his next move.

Caldwell was caught; it was up to Austin to get him out. Nothing to work with but himself, his gun—and the door he had come through. In a sudden whirling motion, he kicked at it with all his strength. There was one hell of a smashing crashing explosion as the metal door crunched in at the blow. He never took his eyes off the two figures up on the next level and halfway across the room from him. While they were distracted by the noise, he got off two rounds at them. The first shot got the closer man in the shoulder, the second hit him again in the chest, slamming him backward. There was one hell of a crash as he plowed backward through the glass wall of the control shack.

Caldwell didn't waste a millisecond; he was out of the trap and away the instant he heard the pistol fire. He crouched down so the conveyor belt was between him and them, took aim, and let off three quick rounds. The second man pitched sideways along the catwalk.

Austin looked down at Caldwell, who was looking up at him with something faintly resembling a smile. Then he looked away and started to move cautiously along a narrow aisle of machinery. Covering him, Austin hunkered down in a crouch and managed to scoot along the narrow catwalk around the corner and over to the control shack. The man he shot was lying half in and half out of the enclosure, which was no longer an enclosure, but a pond of broken glass. There was a lot of blood. The man didn't move, not anymore.

Austin looked inside the shack at the large control panel. He threw a red switch marked ON/OFF from off to on, and then he hit a series of relays. The enormous assembly line below hummed into life. The bottles started to march in single file along the turns and straightaways of the conveyor belt tracks. Austin, still crouching, worked his way further along the catwalk. He had to climb over the dead guy. Caldwell maneuvered himself along underneath the conveyor belt, as the single-file rows of large plastic bottles, glinting in the refracted rays of dying sun, marched over his head as snappily as any unit that ever graced a military parade ground. Except for their orderly rumble, the huge room was suddenly, ominously, hushed. Someone had just cut the alarm. Someone who would *not* be glad to see Austin and Caldwell. Tensely, they continued on their methodical prowl.

Just as Austin came up onto the second glass control shack, a blast hit the window about six inches from where he teetered on the narrow catwalk. The size of the blowout was so huge it had to be from a shotgun, but by the time Austin put that together he had already completed his head-first dive along the walk to the stairwell on the opposite wall from the one he had come in on. Glass from the window was still showering down when a second shotgun blast came through, this one knocking sparks clear into the stairwell a step ahead of him.

There was no time to run down the stairs. Austin ducked under the railing and jumped the ten feet to the ground, just as a third hit exploded a series of bottles uncomfortably close to his ear. He hit the floor and rolled under a giant piece of machinery.

His chin scraping the concrete floor, Austin peered through a slot in the heavyware and checked around to find Caldwell. He had made his way clear over to the other side of the plant. From his cover under the conveyor belt, Caldwell took aim at something up on the catwalk—Austin craned his neck painfully and spotted, through the metal grating of the catwalk, the guy with the shotgun. He was moving along right past the spot where Austin had been standing twenty seconds before. The guy was moving toward the stairwell—and Austin.

He'd seen enough; he started moving. There wasn't enough room under the machines for a man to crawl, but he managed to do it anyway. He was scraping his elbows and knees and chest and chin and probably rubbing the top of his head stone bald, the way it felt, but he couldn't stay in one place, that was for damned sure. He lost sight of Caldwell, hoping the colonel had a bead on the guy and not the other way around.

Austin heard a huge plastic bottle go crashing across the floor, from Caldwell's side of the plant— deliberate, he hoped. He looked up quickly—the man on the catwalk was distracted, turning the shotgun in the direction of the clatter. Caldwell leaped out from behind his cover and fired. The man was hit. He tumbled back, teetered on the rail for an agonizing second, and then crashed over the side onto the conveyor. He was wearing overalls with the logo of Travis Air Force Base, Maintenance. They had seen him earlier in the day. The conveyor belt carried his body along like so many bottles, so much crumpled passenger baggage, another slab of meat for the cooler.

"Yo, Colonel, move it!" The shout came from the opposite side of the room, behind one of the three enormous storage tanks. Caldwell moved it, obeying the call instinctively, before he recognized the voice.

"Maclure!" Caldwell had ducked under the conveyor belt again. His call ricocheted through the plant. A storm of automatic bullets peppered the area where his voice came from, hitting bottles on the moving belt like clay pigeons in a shooting gallery. Caldwell would have been the pigeon if Maclure hadn't made the save.

But giving away his position cost Maclure the big one. Mark Wallach had given up the little gun from his pocket; somewhere he had picked up an automatic and now he was using it. He and Maclure had been standing together, but the top sergeant had fast put the storage tanks between him and the kid. Wallach whirled and turned the automatic toward Maclure's voice, strafing the tanks and all the machinery and walls and windows in the vicinity. Maclure was hit. He spun around and backward. He fell out of sight and rolled under a huge metal stamper that turned flat plastic disks into bottle caps. It was stamping away now, although there was no one to feed it. There was only Maclure, lying very still below the spitting steel tongue and rhythmically turning gears. The pearl-handled .45 fell out of his hand.

Austin was on the other side of the plant, positioned against a wall. He wanted to work his way around back to the staircase and get up to the catwalk where he would have the advantage. But first he had to figure out a way around a mountain of crated and stacked water bottles. Peale's best boy was quiet for now, just watching and waiting for some movement. Getting past the stacked bottles meant stepping out in plain sight. And where was Caldwell—never lose track of your buddy, that was the second most important thing the Army taught you, right after loving your rifle.

He didn't have time to look. Mark Wallach stepped out into the open, firing the automatic as he moved, spraying the wall where Austin crouched. Bottles of water exploded, with bits of plastic shooting into the air and torrents of expensive water pouring down like the days of the Flood. Austin went with the deluge, rolling out of the way just inches from the steady hail of bullets. He dove down behind a piece of machinery, out of sight of Wallach, who disappeared back into his own hiding place. Abruptly, everything was quiet again, except for the water streaming down onto the floor toward a center drain.

Austin continued his slow crawl along the wall toward the staircase. There was a huge barrel between the door and the corner; he could duck behind that if he could navigate the bare space of wall between here and there.

But Mark Wallach was inching his way along the wall, too—toward the same staircase, from the opposite direction. Austin didn't see him. Just as he pushed at the steel door leading into the stairwell, Wallach got off another round. The door caught the fire and bounced back lightning streaks of rapid explosions. Austin fell back and rolled out of the way. He saw Wallach then, moving in closer, heading for the door to the stairway.

Austin ducked behind the barrel. Wallach moved in slowly, edging along the wall. His eyes were on the steel door. Catlike, silent, Austin pulled back toward the conveyor belt, ducking behind stacks of bottles and leaping over the shredded plastic remains and rivulets that made the floor a treacherous place, especially if you were in a hurry.

He looked back at Wallach, who was moving in on the staircase door with something like a smile on his shit-eating face. He thought he had Austin cornered behind the barrel. He took aim and ran with confidence toward the door. Once there, he let fly along the wall behind the barrel where Austin was supposed to be.

Austin jumped up onto the conveyor belt a couple of feet behind Wallach. The jerk stopped shooting. It had finally occurred to him that Austin wasn't hiding behind the barrel.

"Wrong," Austin said. Wallach turned on one heel and Austin squeezed two rounds that hit him squarely in the chest. He jumped down off the belt that was conveying him toward a machine that would have poured a few gallons of water down his neck. He went over to Wallach, checked his pulse, and decided to leave the automatic there; the guy wasn't ever going to hurt anybody with it again.

Now where was Caldwell? Austin hopped on the conveyor belt again. As it headed for the filling machine, he reflexively checked out the details: a series of windows inside the huge machinery. Caldwell was walking cautiously alongside the fillers, but he couldn't see what was lurking inside. Austin had a different vantage point.

"Inside the filler!" he shouted.

The man he had been following all that day reacted fast. From inside the machine, Spota fired his shotgun directly at Caldwell. The windows of the filling machine blew out, but this deflected the blast so that he missed hitting the target. The next shot was courtesy of Caldwell—he hit one of the main water lines to the tank. An ocean of water burst out in a stream forceful enough to knock Caldwell off his feet. He slammed onto the concrete floor, looking like a submarine that had been hit by a depth charge. The whole area filled with water. Caldwell got to his hands and knees. The water was ankle deep and rising fast.

Austin shot at Spota over and over again, but he was completely protected by the machinery. Now Spota moved out of the filling machine to draw a closer bead on Caldwell, leaving the machine between him and the advancing Austin, who could do nothing at this point, nothing at all.

Caldwell got to his feet in the swirling water. He saw Spota and fired. Zilch. An empty click was all he got. No bullets. Then Spota fired. The shotgun blast was deafening. It ripped a hole a foot wide in the wall next to Caldwell's head. He dove for cover into the water, now about knee high. He pushed over to the machine, wedged himself against it. He had Caldwell trapped.

Austin had two choices: he could swing around and try to catch Spota from behind, meaning he would be splashing around loudly with absolutely nowhere to hide; or he could make for the staircase now and get the advantage from above. He couldn't reach Spota from where he stood, and Caldwell needed something positive to happen, right now. Austin jumped off the belt into the water, made his way as quietly as he could to the stairwell door, desperately bargaining with whatever powers that be to give Caldwell some kind of edge until he was in position to help him.

Spota had the same idea. He was making for the stairs on the other side of the room, closer to the filling machine. Caldwell lay low until Spota went through the door. Then he moved fast, over to an aisle between the conveyor and the capping machine, an area not so visible from above. The aisle was filling with water. Some of the water was bloody. At the end of the aisle, propped against the wall, ex-Sergeant Major Maclure sat, half-dazed, his shoulder a bloody mess. He was drenched in water, sweat, and blood, all running together.

Austin had reached the catwalk; so had Spota, on the other side of the plant. Spota took aim at Caldwell. Austin took a shot at Spota, but the shotgun had already gone off. Caldwell had no gun, all he could do was duck. Keeping both eyes on Spota, he moved closer to Maclure, who was holding on to his bloody shoulder and wincing.

"Looks like we're back in the shit again, Colonel," he said.

Caldwell nodded. "In the name of Christ, why?" he asked.

Maclure took his hand away from the fragmented bone that stuck out of a hole in his flesh. He pointed along the wall. Caldwell looked. His pearl-handled .45 was lying there, out of the damp.

Austin tried to get off another round at Spota, but he came up empty, too. He thought of the automatic lying at the foot of the staircase with Mark Wallach's body. He ducked through the door and hit the stairs like a downhill racer. Spota fired at Caldwell again, just grazing his head, enough to keep Caldwell from going after the pistol.

"Damn!"

"It was my screw-up," Maclure told him. "It doesn't matter why anymore."

Spota fired again. Caldwell was spending most of this time flat on his belly and mostly submerged, crawling toward the .45.

"I'm going to make things right," Maclure said.

Caldwell looked at him. Suddenly he knew what Maclure was saying. "No, don't!" he pleaded.

Maclure managed a smile. "Funny, ain't it?" he said. "What a difference five minutes can make?"

He got painfully to his feet. Caldwell reached up to pull him back, but Spota shot off another round and he fell back. An unending round of fire can keep you low and slow. It was suicide to move. With horror, he watched Maclure stand there and then begin to slog through the water to the high ground at the wall. Spota fired. The blast hit Maclure in the side, spinning him around. Guts and tissue and blood spurted through his Polo shirt. He was mortally wounded, but he kept staggering forward. There was another kind of shot— Austin with the automatic now, spraying Spota, but not in range for him, shooting from clear across the room and ineffective against the shotgun. Austin would have to move in closer. Maclure got another blast to the midsection, almost cutting him in half. How did the old man keep going? But he did. He reached down and, with a terrible groan, picked up the gun. With his last breath, Maclure flung the .45 to Caldwell, who caught it neatly. Maclure fell in a horrible heap and didn't move again.

The instant the gun was in his hand, Caldwell dove back into the water. As Spota adjusted his aim, Caldwell started firing up at him. All three guns were going at the same instant: Austin at Spota, Spota at Caldwell, Caldwell at Spota. Caldwell emptied his gun, in a mixture of grief and rage.

Spota twitched with the impact of the bullets; his lifeless form catapulted over the railing and fell with a final thump onto the concrete floor.

Caldwell pulled himself to his feet, amazed that all his parts seemed to be still working. He couldn't remember ever being this exhausted before in his life. He went over to Maclure and stood looking down at him, sadly. And then all hell broke loose all over again.

Automatic weapon fire blasted away from the main aisle of the plant. With less than seconds between him and extinction, Caldwell's instincts took over and he was down on his belly again. What an idiot he'd been, forgetting Arthur Peale. The tycoon was standing in full view, taking careful aim. He was setting his sights a tad lower, ready to fire again to take off Caldwell's head.

Austin didn't take time to think. He vaulted over the catwalk rail down onto the top of the capping machine, hitting it in full stride. He sprang forward, almost the way Tarzan used to swing from vine to vine in the jungle. He grabbed hold of a pipe and hurtled himself forward to another machine, and then he dove headfirst onto the conveyor belt at the point where the rollers were slanting toward the back of the building and the loading docks.

Peale hardly had time to figure out what was happening. Austin slid down the conveyor belt on his stomach, his gun pointing straight ahead. During the entire slide, he was pushing that trigger, emptying the entire magazine of fourteen shots at Peale.

As the belt brought the gunfire closer and closer, Peale started shooting back at Austin. Bottles exploded with irregular frequency, sounding not unlike mortars in the distance, spraying expensive water everywhere. Austin just kept sliding and firing until the magazine was empty. Peale was hit—more than once. His chest was punctured with bloody holes that rapidly grew larger. Suddenly he was flung back against the wall where bottles were lined up ready for pickup. He knocked against them, sending a few crates clattering down. He slumped to the streaming floor.

Austin reached the end of the roller-coaster slide and landed on his hands and feet. He quickly straightened up and went over to take a close look at Peale's body. Very dead.

He looked back for Caldwell. "Caldwell! You okay?" he shouted, not seeing him.

Caldwell answered from behind the filling machine. "Yes. You?"

"Fine and dandy," Austin said. He picked his way through the floating plastic river. When he reached the narrow aisle behind the filler, he saw the blood on the water and then he saw Maclure. Caldwell was standing over his body. There was a terrible look of pain on the colonel's face. Austin felt embarrassed, as if he'd caught him in a highly personal act.

Caldwell looked up at Austin. "I want you to do something for me," he said.

"What?"

"Delay your report forty-eight hours. That will give me time to bury him with his name still—I mean . . . whatever he did, he deserves that."

Austin didn't say anything. He just looked at the colonel. Army was asking to evade regulations. It was a big thing to ask. It would put the colonel into the definitely human category, and give Austin something over him, if he was the kind of bastard who would take an advantage like that, which he wasn't. It occurred to him that Caldwell was putting his life in Austin's hands. You might say that.

"Please," Caldwell said.

Austin nodded. "Okay," he said quietly.

CHAPTER 17

It was a beautiful day, brightly sunny but with a crisp edge to the warmth. Birds sang and the Golden Gate rose like a monument at the head of the bay. Rolling green hillsides, dotted with white gravestones, baked in the sun.

Near a granite spire, several rows of officers and enlisted men in dress uniforms sat solemnly on folding chairs. There were some civilians there, too. Donna and Austin sat in the front row.

An officer and a six-man honor guard in dress blues, saucer caps, white gloves, and pistol belts, watched over a flag-draped coffin, standing at attention during the entire ceremony. They stood under a white canopy that shielded the coffin from the direct rays of the sun. Each man carried an M-16 on a wide white shoulder strap.

Farther off, a six-man firing squad, also carrying M-16s, awaited their signal for the final salute.

Lt. Col. Alan Caldwell, Sixth Army Provost Marshal, The Presidio, San Francisco, stepped up to the podium facing the orderly rows of mourners. Above and behind his head, the monument had an eagle carved into its smooth spire. On the eagle's breast, in bold relief: **TO THE UNKNOWN DEAD**.

Donna sat like a statue. She was thinking of the walk they had taken here only days before and wondered if Top had had a premonition. Her father's voice began to echo through the cemetery, not disturbing the deep peace there but reaffirming all the rites and ceremonies which had taken place on this hallowed ground.

Austin sat beside her. He wanted to hold her hand, to reach out and let her know he was there for her, because he knew she'd lost someone closer than a friend. But this was between her and her dad and Maclure. He sat quietly and listened to Caldwell as he spoke about . . . well, love.

"None of us who knew Sergeant Major Ross Maclure could ever accuse him of being perfect," Caldwell said. He had to clear his throat before he could go on. "However, only God can judge him now. I won't. Nor will I apologize for him."

He wasn't looking directly at Austin, but he was talking right to him.

"He was my friend. He was a soldier. We used to joke that being in the Army isn't a matter of life and death. It's more important than that."

A gentle wind rippled through the trees. Some of the low leafy branches seemed to kneel down to the hallowed earth of the quiet cemetery. Caldwell stopped; he was hunting for words. A shiver went through Donna, despite the warmth of the early afternoon. She had never seen her father so moved.

"We first met in Vietnam," he went on finally. "He was my sergeant, I was his lieutenant. To this day, I don't know who served under whom. It was his luck to be a hero in a war that nobody liked. He once said to me that winning his medal was a lot easier than . . . wearing it."

He stopped to swallow.

"One day when we were in Saigon, he took me to see an old lady who sold wild canaries in bamboo cages. The thing was that you couldn't keep the birds. What you paid for was the experience of opening the cage and setting the canary free. Maclure loved the whole idea. I thought it was a waste of time. I was wrong."

Donna's eyes filled with tears. Austin glanced at her and saw the way she looked. There were only two people in the world for her right now—herself and her father. Austin thought he loved her more in this minute than in all the wild loving times they'd had so far and would have again.

"This is the second time I've lost someone who meant everything," Caldwell said simply. "Whenever I come to visit this place, all I can hear is the silence, and the sense of loss. Maclure told me he heard something else."

Caldwell looked straight into his daughter's eyes. He nodded, privately, and she lifted her chin and nodded back. Yes, he told me, too. Maybe he's already having his long peaceful talk with the corporal from the Spanish-American War. I hope so.

"I hope he was right," Caldwell said, echoing her thoughts. "There are so many things I wish I had said to him . . . about . . . because . . . well, it just would have been nice. Now that he's gone," he went on, looking straight at his daughter, "I realize that things should not be left unsaid . . . even between people who don't easily say them."

Tears rolled down Donna's cheeks. She reached to take Austin's hand and held it tightly. He was terribly moved, by the words, by the way Caldwell and Donna were making everything right between them, by her knowing he was there for her. It was all of those things, and mourning the loss of a good man, whatever he had done. It was all mixed up together. Austin couldn't sort it all out now, not by himself. He clung as tightly to Donna's hand as she did to his.

Caldwell cleared his throat again. Glancing at the coffin, he said, simply, "So here we are . . . in this place that he loved so much. We are here to say good-bye. And, if I know the sergeant major, he's impatient to be on his way."

He saluted the coffin. "Good-bye, old friend," he said.

It was over. The bugler played taps. The rifle squad got off the final salute. I forgot to mention that he won the country's highest medal, Caldwell thought as the shots reverberated on the balmy afternoon breeze. He walked over to the coffin. All the officers and enlisted men stood.

Two of the Honor Guard folded the flag, just so. Caldwell saluted again. The men in uniform did the same. Two other young men of the Honor Guard took the flag, handed it to Caldwell.

"On behalf of the United States of America and a grateful nation, please accept these colors," the sergeant major said.

The participants turned to leave. Caldwell walked over to Donna and Austin, who were standing alone, holding hands. He held out the flag to his daughter. "Donna . . . I'd like you to have this," he said.

She put both hands out to receive the flag. She was trembling visibly. Tears cascaded down her cheeks, unchecked. Her father looked down at her with great love and tenderness and concern. "You want to go for a walk?" he asked her, tentatively.

Grabbing the flag in one hand, she hugged her father very close. "I'd like that very much," she said.

Caldwell grinned and took her hand. They turned just a half step and then Caldwell stopped and looked back at Austin. "Come on," he said.

Donna kissed his cheek impetuously and then held out her other hand to Austin. He grabbed it, took the flag from her, and carried it carefully. They moved off together.

Behind, at half-mast, Old Glory crackled and popped in the wind.